*Passion and
Compassion
Collide on . . .*

Passion and Compassion Collide on . . .

a novel by
Robert Sikkenga
Author of *Moon Over Ajalon*

© 2005 by Robert Sikkenga. All rights reserved

Second Edition

Pleasant Word (a division of WinePress Publishing, PO Box 428, Enumclaw, WA 98022) functions only as book publisher. As such, the ultimate design, content, editorial accuracy, and views expressed or implied in this work are those of the author.

No part of this publication may be reproduced, stored in a retrieval system or transmitted in any way by any means—electronic, mechanical, photocopy, recording or otherwise—without the prior permission of the copyright holder, except as provided by USA copyright law.

Unless otherwise noted, all Scriptures are taken from the Holy Bible, New International Version, Copyright © 1973, 1978, 1984 by the International Bible Society. Used by permission of Zondervan Publishing House. The "NIV" and "New International Version" trademarks are registered in the United States Patent and Trademark Office by International Bible Society.

Scripture references marked KJV are taken from the King James Version of the Bible.

Scripture references marked NASB are taken from the New American Standard Bible, © 1960, 1963, 1968, 1971, 1972, 1973, 1975, 1977 by The Lockman Foundation. Used by permission.

ISBN 1-4141-0413-8
Library of Congress Catalog Card Number: 2005901507

Table of Contents

Chapter 1: The Gun 1
Chapter 2: Cass White...4
Chapter 3: Memphis...11
Chapter 4: The Neighborhood............................23
Chapter 5: Hickey 29
Chapter 6: Albert...37
Chapter 7: Professor Bisschop 41
Chapter 8: The Necessity of Pious Living..............47
Chapter 9: Josie La Farge.....................................52
Chapter 10: Neighbors 58
Chapter 11: A Sanctified Suit 63
Chapter 12: Anything for a Neighbor 71
Chapter 13: wiskie for edwerd 77
Chapter 14: The Only Flaw in Paradise 80
Chapter 15: The Only Tenderness 87
Chapter 16: Sunday at Calvin's 91
Chapter 17: A Glass of Tea 99
Chapter 18: A Family Thing................................104

Chapter 19: Soldiers of the Cross 110
Chapter 20: The Fourth of July 115
Chapter 21: You Ain't No Man! 125
Chapter 22: Serves Him Right! 129
Chapter 23: Your Fellow Drunkard 134
Chapter 24: The Hore of Babbylin......................140
Chapter 25: Like the 'Postle Paul 146
Chapter 26: A Proper Field..................................153
Chapter 27: Alone on the Sidewalk 156
Chapter 28: A Prince of a Man 163
Chapter 29: Mysterious Ways..............................166
Chapter 30: The Wisdom of Solomon 169
Chapter 31: A Stately Event.................................174
Chapter 32: Where Tulips Once Bloomed 177
Chapter 33: The Gun 180

A Short Story: Legion A Man Possessed 184

Cardinal Error 211

Ashes..215

CHAPTER ONE

The Gun

When I entered the police station, the overweight, balding sergeant sitting at a desk turned in his swivel chair and rose to meet me at the counter.

"May I help you sir?"

I noticed his nametag. "Dowd?" I asked. "When I was a kid here in Hackley, I knew a Dowd family from Amity Street... any relation?"

"My dad was a policeman back then, John Dowd."

"Are you Jackie Dowd?" I asked, squinting at him to discern the face of the youngster I once knew.

"Yah. I'm Jack Dowd. And you? Your face is familiar, but...." He peered at me intently.

"Chris Newmyer." I reached out and shook his hand.

"Chris Newmyer! Golly! Good to see you again. Your hair is different and you're not so skinny no more. I guess we've both changed a lot. How long has it been?"

"Probably back in high school."

"What are you doing now?"

"I work for a newspaper in Detroit. I write features."

"Did you come back to Hackley to write a story about your old home town?"

"No, but I think I might have stumbled on one. Let me show you." I opened the manila envelope, took out the gun, and handed it to him.

He looked at the gun. "A little single shot twenty-two. Haven't seen one of these in years. You can hide it in the palm of your hand. So small we can frisk a guy and not notice it. Black guys used to carry 'em in the old days. My dad took a few off the boys down at the Sepia. That old hangout is still there down at the foot of Pine Street. Old Wash Giles died some time back and his son Isaac runs the place now. Nasty place these days. We're bustin' it all the time. Whores… gambling…."

He talked on. "Cass White used to drink down there every day when we was kids. Remember how he used to stagger back down Amity Street drunk and lose his way? We used to have to corral him until Queen Anne could come and fetch him home. I wonder whatever became of her after he died."

"Well Jack, some of your answers might be right here in this envelope. I think I'm here to report a murder, that is if it matters anymore." I didn't say that I knew a lot more than I was telling right then.

He looked at me with a quizzical furl on his forehead. I handed him the folded note I'd found in the envelope with the gun.

He read it slowly. "So the old sot got shot! That's a new wrinkle. I looked for a file when I first come on the job. There's hardly no record here at all except that they buried him out there by the old poor farm. Gee! I remember it well. Got woke up by the fire trucks. Old number two came clanging by our house. Hell of a fire! Don't you remember, Chris, we stood there together and watched it burn."

"Yes, Jack, I remember as if it were yesterday."

"I remember them dragging his roasted carcass out in a body bag and throwing it in the back of Otis Blake's pickup. So the old sot got shot. I wonder who done it...."

CHAPTER TWO

Cass White

"Some say he got beaned by a high hard one during his rookie season in the Negro League," my dad told me one day when I asked him about Cass's head, "others say he got whacked during a race riot in Memphis."

Cass White's face was dented just above his left cheekbone and his eye bulged out. My dad allowed the former cause for his deformity because he said that when they were kids, "He was the best baseball player I ever seen. If he only was a white man he could have made the big leagues. He's a pretty decent guy, drunk or sober. I don't think he'd get involved in a riot."

Cass lived on my street, Wood Street, just a couple blocks north of Amity, a half block down the hill in the neighborhood the more refined called the Negro Section, but which those among us who were less considerate called "nigger town."

Cass White

There were two Cass Whites. The morning Cass and the afternoon Cass. The morning Cass was a quiet, respectable man who devoted his time to teaching young boys the finer points of baseball. Every morning during summer vacation, Cass and his select group of high school boys gathered in the old Angell School play yard for instruction. The old school had long since been torn down and practically the whole city block had become a vacant lot that the school board had been trying to sell for years, but there were no buyers because it was in a "bad location" right on the edge of the Negro Section. There Cass taught Hackley's best young athletes how to hit and field, pitch, and run the bases.

"He's a great teacher," Mr. Benton, the head of the Veterans' Association Youth League, used to say, "too bad he got beaned and can't see too good no more. He could have been a great one." Cass would stand at home plate wearing his old Memphis Red Sox baseball cap and hit crisp grounders to the infielders. Sometimes he would shout, "double play," and smack one to the shortstop who would scoop it up and toss it to the second baseman, who would step on the bag and fire it to first. Sometimes he would hit a liner or a fly to the outfield, never telegraphing his intent, making sure all the players were "on their toes." His swing was easy, his gait relaxed and his stride perfectly coordinated. His orders were terse and authoritarian. No one ever purposely did anything to offend him for fear of being cut from his "team."

His "team" never played any games. They gathered at the school yard purely for instruction and only because they had a note from their youth league coach identifying them as young men of extraordinary talent. He coached Dutch boys from my neighborhood, including my neighbor, Donny Eldersveld, Italian boys from the neighborhood behind Hackley Motor Works, Polish boys from across Apple Street and Black boys from his own neighborhood. I swear the double play combination of Clanton to Eldersveld to Panozzo would someday become as much a cliché as Tinker to Evers to Chance, that is if they ever let Black players into the major leagues, or even into the youth league here in Hackley.

One thing that was assumed as natural back then, but that stands out in retrospect as monumentally inhumane, is that only white boys had teams that played competitively in the youth league. The Dutch boys had a team sponsored by Veldema's Hardware. Petrone's Grocery sponsored the Italians, and Seradski's Used Cars sponsored the Polish team. But the Black players had no sponsor. The only Black-owned business capable of sponsoring a team was the Sepia Club, but the moral dictates of the day would not allow a tavern to sponsor a team in the youth league. Petrone's was okay because they sold groceries as well as alcohol. Since no white-owned business would sponsor them, the Black kids who lived down Wood Street and up toward Pine could only practice with Cass, sometimes playing games among themselves or against kids who couldn't make it onto teams in the league. And nobody cared.

Cass also taught character. Those of us who were too young to play but who hoped someday to catch Cass's attention would bring our gloves and play catch behind the homemade wood and chicken wire backstop, showing off our skills. When he taught pitching, we would watch from behind the backstop. Cass could toss a ball up and hit it anywhere he wanted to blindfolded, just by feel, but because of his impaired vision he didn't dare throw, so he taught pitching by standing behind the pitcher's box and talking to the boy on the mound who would throw to players who were taking batting practice.

Some mornings Mr. Benton would stand and watch with us. He and Cass were good friends, having played pickup ball together in their youth. "You youngsters listen to everything Cass says," he often reminded those of us who were spectators, "if you want to play in the league when you get older. He was the best shortstop I ever seen, and he's the best coach I ever seen."

Once, while standing behind the backstop next to Mr. Benton, I saw Sonny Clanton's brother, Lincoln, intentionally throw a high inside burner to Steve Pulaski, brushing him back from the plate and forcing him to hit the dirt.

"Oh oh. Watch this," Mr. Benton said, "Cass is really mad now."

Cass grabbed Lincoln by the arm, dragged him off the field and sat him down very firmly on the bench.

"Don't you never do that again," he warned. "We don't never bursh back nobody! You could hurt him bad, or even kill him. Besides, if you gotta bursh back a batter to get him skeert of you, you ain't no kind of pitcher. Now sit right here 'til we be done, then git on home and don't come back until nex' week. Yer lucky you ain't gone for good." Lincoln slumped on the ground behind the backstop and hung his head. He never threw a bean ball again.

Color and nationality meant nothing to Cass. A boy was a boy and he judged him solely on his character and ability. Though he had to play ball in a segregated league, live in a segregated corner of town and drink beer in a segregated bar, he had faith that someday all of that would change. He created in his Black players a hope that they could someday play for the Yankees or the Tigers, but if they couldn't, to be content playing for the Memphis Red Sox or the Kansas City Monarchs in the Negro League, as he had done. If it was good enough for the likes of Josh Gibson, Buck Leonard and Satchel Paige, it should be good enough for them, he said. None of us could possibly imagine that the Jackie Robinson era was just a few years away, or that it could have been Cass instead of Jackie.

As soon as the noon whistle blew at Hackley Motor Works, Cass ended practice and left the field, stopping first at home to eat a quick lunch, kiss Queen Anne goodbye and change from his baseball cap into an old fedora, then walking west toward the Sepia Club, which marked the end of Amity Street at the corner of

Pine. He walked lightly and erect, with determination, lips drawn tight and eyes straight ahead, except for his bulging left eye, which sometimes wandered a bit, as if unattached to anything inside his skull.

Just before suppertime he staggered toward home, reeling in an ungainly manner from side to side, disheveled, slouched over, hat atilt, lower lip hanging and drooling, and fly usually open. Being disoriented when he was drunk, he often turned right into the Dutch Section instead of left toward his own house when he got to Wood Street.

"Chuckie, go get Queen Anne," I would shout as I saw him make the wrong turn on to Wood Street. Then Calvin VandeBruin, Jackie Dowd and I would form a moving barricade with our bikes in front of Elder Doorn's grocery store to corral Cass and keep him from straying any deeper into the Dutch neighborhood, while Chuckie Eldersveld, Donny's younger brother, raced to Cass's house to fetch Queen Anne. I think Cass never did us any harm because he knew Jackie Dowd's dad was a cop.

Elder Doorn often strode out the front door of his store brandishing a broom and ordering Cass to turn around and go the other way, "Get back where you belong, boy!" Elder Doorn would shout, shaking his broom at him, "You're forgetting your place."

When we blocked his way, Cass got irritated, but not violent. "Git outa my road," he would mumble as we maneuvered our bikes into his erratic path, and as Elder Doorn prodded him in the stomach with the straw end of the broom. He hollered "Hesh ep!" when we tried to tell him that he lived in the other direction. He seemed to know where he wanted to go, but had no idea where he was.

Queen Anne would soon arrive, gently take his hand and say, "Come on Casien, come home with Lovie," and he would obediently turn and walk by her side in the opposite direction while she glanced back, gave us all a sad, apologetic look and murmured, "Thank you, boys."

Back then we didn't know what Queen Anne's real name was. Some said it was really Queen Anne, others said that they had heard Cass call her Josie. Rumor was that he met her in a night club in Memphis when he played for the Red Sox there, and that after he got beaned she stuck by him and took care of him until he could get better. But he never got better. He took to drink. And the word *alcoholic* not being in the Dutch vocabulary, Cass White was simply called a drunk.

Queen Anne was a pretty lady, petite, light skinned, with long, straight black hair, and a few freckles under her eyes. She always wore dresses, dark dresses as if not to stand out. Some said she quit singing in the Memphis nightclub because it was run by gamblers and pimps who abused her. Good Dutch ladies considerately called her his common law wife, and condescendingly said of him, "He drinks, you know."

CHAPTER THREE

Memphis

"Ya gotta wear a coat and tie in The Oasis," the doorman grunted. "If you ain't got one, you can borrow one of ours... for a quarter."

So when Josie La Farge first laid eyes on Cass White he was wearing a jacket that didn't match his trousers and an ugly tie that clashed with his shirt. He was such a funny sight that she almost forgot the words of the song she was crooning into the microphone as he fumbled through the darkness and the haze of the Memphis nightclub to find a vacant table. Finding none, he perched on a bar stool at the far end of the stage.

Mesmerized by the earthy tone of her voice as she crooned the sad words of a blues song, he gazed intently at her. And she gazed back, not because he looked so odd and out of place, but because she detected a sincerity in his eyes and an earnestness in his face that contrasted sharply with the pretense belied by the smiles, handshakes and back pats of the better dressed men in the club.

"Buy a lady a drink, mistah?" she said as she stood beside him after finishing her set, her silky crimson gown rendering his appearance even more grotesque. Others sitting nearby grinned and rolled their eyes.

"I spent all my money just to get in here and buy one beer," he responded.

"Okay then, I just put it on my tab."

Cass slowly sipped his beer while she nursed her ginger ale with a cherry in the bottom of the glass. "I'm a ball player for the Red Sox," he offered proudly as he introduced himself. "The guys say I should come to The Oasis if I want to meet a nice girl."

"You can meet a girl here if you want to, but they mostly not nice ones, if you know what I mean by nice. If you want to meet a really nice girl you orta come to the New Jerusalem Baptist Church." Just then Mr. Moe, the proprietor of The Oasis stepped between them and in a demanding tone told her to find more appropriate company with whom to drink. "You be at the church Sunday mornin' now, at nine o'clock" she insisted as she glided away. "I be there lookin' for you."

He watched her as she approached a well groomed man with straightened and slicked down hair sitting at a table alone. He returned her smile and she sat next to him, dutifully talking and laughing as he ordered her a drink. Cass noticed the ambiance of the room: tobacco smoke mixed with a sweet trace of something he had never smelled before, an overpowering clash of perfumes, colognes and aftershaves, and a swirling halo effect created by the spotlights and the revolving ball accompanied by the moan of a saxophone and the swishing of silk. "Never see nothin' like this before," he whispered to himself. Then he said, "These ain't my kind of folk" loud enough for the man next to him to hear. Removing the borrowed tie and the jacket as he groped his way to the entrance through the maze of tables, Cass White went back to the boarding house where some of the Red Sox lived.

On Sunday morning he made his way to the New Jerusalem Baptist church, avoided the greeters at the door and slipped into the back row wearing a pair of shiny black pants, a borrowed bow tie and a white shirt frayed a bit at the cuffs. He looked around but didn't see her, then he slouched down into the pew hoping that the ladies parading by in their colorful dresses and their big, fancy hats with veils and the men in starched shirts and expensive suits with wide lapels wouldn't notice him.

When the church was nearly full, the choir entered from a side door, and there she was, in the front row, swaying, dancing, and clapping as the white-robed singers chanted their way up onto the stage. He could hear her clearly, not singing in the same sultry voice of The Oasis, but in a crisp soprano, and not the blues but a lively gospel tune.

His eyes were fastened on her through the entire service, and he hardly heard the pastor's sermon extolling the first church in old Jerusalem in which the members held "all things in common," and asserting that the members of the New Jerusalem Baptist Church should, in the words of Jesus, "go and do likewise."

He lingered in the narthex when the service ended, waiting for her to come down the aisle. Instead she slipped in from a basement stairway and surprised him from behind with a playful "boo!" and a poke in both ribs with fingers softer and gentler than any he had ever felt.

"Come to my house for dinner," she urged, in a tone completely different than the seductive voice of The Oasis, "We 'spectin' you, and Mama done cook enough for the whole carnagation."

With a nod he assented with the added specification that he had to be back to the ball park by one o'clock.

As they walked the three blocks through the shabby business district to where she lived, he got up the courage to say, "You be two different peoples. At the nightclub you be a Jezzybel in a red dress, but in church you be a angel. How come?"

"Well," she answered, "a girl do gotta make a livin' and we gotta do what Mr. Moe say. He say happy mens come back for more. He want me to wear red dresses. He say it good for business. I say 'ho's wear red dresses,' and he say 'you can look like a 'ho and not be one'."

"Who Mr. Moe?"

"He own the place, and us girls gotta get the mens to buy us drinks. We just get ginger ale, but the mens pay like we drinkin' Martinis. That how Mr. Moe get rich. And some of the girls is 'ho's and Mr. Moe get a cut of they action. They use his room upstairs."

"You sing pretty. I like that, but not the other stuff."

"Once Mr. Moe try to get me to go upstairs with one of the mens who was spendin' lots of money. I say no and he get mad. He told me that if I don't, the man might not come back, and I told him that if the man want to hear me sing he either gotta come back to The Oasis or come to church. He ain't bother me since, but he ain't been nice to me neither."

"I don't even know what your name be. At The Oasis they call you Queen something."

"They call me Queen Anne at The Oasis, but my real name is Josie Anne LaFarge. I grow up here in Me'phis. I don't know your name neither."

"Cass. Cass White. It really Casien, but ever'body just call me Cass."

"I like Casien," she said with firmness. "I call you Casien."

"And what I call you?"

"Josie. Just Josie. I like Josie."

Josie and her mother lived in a tiny apartment over the hardware store. At dinner Mama did most of the talking as she served her special fried chicken with buttermilk biscuits, mashed potatoes and gravy. Cass and Josie said little, but looked at each other across the table during the entire meal with glances that attested to some special warmth that was developing between them in spite of their differences.

Mama was big. Real big. Somehow through the hard times she managed to get enough fried chicken, potatoes and biscuits to maintain her obesity.

Mama explained that Josie's father had come up from New Orleans during the depression and got a job in the hardware store. But he had died several years before, and she and her daughter had remained in the small apartment. During the hard times the proprietor, Mr. Hankins, had been generous with them and frequently deferred a portion of the rent when Mama couldn't find anyone to buy the clothes that she had made or if she couldn't collect from the people who owed her for mending their shirts and trousers and coats. Sometimes she treated Mr. and Mrs. Hankins, who lived in the larger apartment next door, to a platter of fried chicken, a treat for which they were always grateful. Mama was as generous to her debtors as her benefactors were to her.

Her pride, and the only special piece of furniture was the well-wrought treadle sewing machine in the corner of the room. Josie's father had purchased it for her at a good price when the hard times hit and some merchants were forced to liquidate as much of their stock as possible just to put food on the table. And at that sewing machine she made her own clothes and taught her daughter the art of dress making.

When Cass rose to leave just in time to make it to the ball park, Josie and Mama urged him to leave his shirt behind so they could launder it and make new cuffs and a collar. When he hesitated, Josie said, with a twinkle, "If you leave it you gotta come back an' git it… and eat more fried chicken." With that he left his only white shirt at the small apartment over the hardware store.

Thus their friendship began in the spring of that extraordinary year. He visited The Oasis once a week and went to church every Sunday when the team was in town, and sometimes Josie went to one of his games and sat in the bleachers. Josie and Mama made him two fine suits, a spiffy one for wearing at The Oasis and a more dignified one for church, and she wouldn't allow him to wear his church suit to The Oasis. "That be a sanctified suit," she declared after his baptism, "and you can't wear it to sinny places." Before the year was half finished, Cass was as at home in the church as he was on the baseball diamond. He was the best shortstop the Red Sox had seen in years, and he soon became somewhat of a celebrity among the sports-minded people of Memphis as well as a celebrity both in the church and at The Oasis.

Just as his rookie season ended, Mama died of a heart attack, and after a brief decent interval Cass gathered up his few belongings, which consisted mainly of his two good suits, a small valise of clothes, his baseball shoes and his glove, and he went to live with Josie in the little apartment over the hardware store. Their choice to move in together was driven both by their affection for each other and by financial necessity, since his weekly paychecks from the team and his rooming house privileges were suspended until spring.

The winter went well. The economy began to improve. Cass took an off-season job at the hardware store sweeping the aisles, stocking the shelves and making deliveries in the store's old pickup truck. Josie made dresses and mended clothes during the day and continued to sing at The Oasis at night. When she sang, Cass took up his usual seat at the end of the bar and slowly sipped his beer. He learned not to mind too much when she sat with other men who enjoyed her conversation while she drank several expensive glasses of ginger ale, but he grew very uncomfortable when they began to get too friendly with her or tried to urge her to go upstairs.

Whenever a customer began to get close to her, Mr. Moe would distract Cass with conversation and would order him another beer... on the house. One time when a stranger began to fondle her, Cass went over to where she was sitting, took her by the hand and led her away. Mr. Moe showed his disapproval by taking her aside and reminding her that it was her job to sell drinks and to keep the customers happy. Then he gripped Cass tightly on his wrist and told him to keep out of his business. "I don't mess with your baseballin', and don't you mess with my nightclubbin'. I be warnin' you now, Cass. I got my ways. Now you jus' sit here and suck down the free beer that me and them baseball fans buy for you and let Queen Anne do her binnes."

At home that night they had their first real argument. Josie declared very firmly that her only purpose at The Oasis was to sing and to "visit decent" with the customers so she could make enough money to help with the rent and life's other necessities. "'Tween us we just get by, and we still got some back rent to pay. I just be doin' my best for bo'f us."

He couldn't argue against that logic, but made it clear that her flirting irked him, "specially when I drink more beer. I get nasty feelin' in the head."

"Then drink ginger ale like I do."

"But I don't like ginger ale and sometime Moe give me free beer now jus' to hesh me up. Other peoples buy me beer too." He began to like the taste and the effect of the beer. It helped him blend in with the aura of the place, and the more he drank the more he began to feel like a regular customer and a celebrity.

In April the season opened and visiting teams came to Memphis to play the Red Sox. The Monarchs had a brash new pitcher named Quincy "Bullet" Buck, who was alleged to be able to throw a ball a hundred miles an hour and hit a tin can sixty feet away. In the first game of the series, Buck pitched a perfect no-hitter and struck Cass out three times with three pitches. He was horribly out of shape. It was the most humiliating day he had ever had at the plate. And he fumbled two grounders he should have fielded.

That night Buck and his Monarch friends invaded The Oasis to celebrate. As Josie sang, Buck blustered his way toward the stage and stood there, at the bottom step, devouring her with his eyes. When she finished singing she stepped off the stage and began to walk toward Cass at the bar. She tried to walk around Buck, but he intercepted her, put his arms around her and began forcefully to dance her around the floor as the music played.

Cass, four beers high from the embarrassment of the day, leaped from his stool and flew headlong into Buck, twisting him around, pulling his arms back and wrestling him to the floor. But Buck, bigger, heavier and stronger than Cass, rolled him over, got on top of him and punched him in the belly with his left hand harder than he had ever been punched in his life. As the cheering crowd gathered around them, Buck's friends pulled him back and Josie went down on her knees beside Cass to protect him. She helped him to his feet just as a few white off-duty policemen stepped forward. But the short fight had already been broken up. Everybody, including the police officers, just laughed.

Except Mr. Moe, that is. He took Cass and Josie each firmly by an arm and ushered them to the door. "Don't neither of you never come back to my place again! You don't do nothin' but cause trouble and cos' me money," he growled through his teeth as he shoved them past the doorman into the street. They walked home, she sobbing, and he cursing quietly under his breath.

The next day was Sunday but they skipped church. She made a breakfast of eggs and corned beef, and they sat closely together in silence, each feeling the other's hurt and shame. In the afternoon he went to the ball park as usual and Josie went along and sat in the bleachers.

In the first inning he bobbled a grounder and made a wild throw to first base. The Monarchs went on to score six runs before their ninth batter came to the plate. To the Red Sox' surprise it was Buck, in the lineup for the second day in a row. Buck hit a double, and as he stood on second base he sneered at Cass. "I ain't neither wore out from yesterday or last night. I gon' make a ass of you again today, boy." The next batter struck out.

Cass led off for the Red Sox. He stood in the box and waited for Buck's first pitch. Buck wound up, lifted his leg high, reared back and fired. The ball came straight at Cass' head and he didn't have the reflexes to move.

The ball crashed into the side of his face just below the eye, and with a bone shattering explosion the lights in his brain flared up brilliantly for just a moment, then went completely out.

Three days later, when the light began to flicker back on, he was in the hospital and Josie was sitting at his side. His head ached, his left eye was totally dark and the vision in his right eye blurred. But he was alive. He never felt the same, he never thought the same, he never understood the same. But he had Josie.

"Lovie gon' take care of you," she whispered over and over again as they walked slowly from the hospital entrance to the street corner. "I don't know how we do it, but Lovie gon' take good care of you."

They took a bus home and he looked at himself in the mirror for the first time. He saw his deformed face, his smashed cheekbone, and his useless eyeball protruding from its socket. "I be a mess," was all he could say. "I be a mess."

A few days later a lawyer from the Negro League came to the apartment and "settled" with Cass. For a hundred and fifty dollars up front and thirty dollars a month for the next ten years he signed an agreement not to pursue the matter further. That was a fortune to a poor man who expected nothing.

Early in June when Cass' head didn't hurt quite so much, he and Josie spent part of their windfall to purchase the hardware's old pickup truck, loaded their few belongings and the sewing machine into the back, covered them with a canvas, and drove north to Hackley where they came to live with Cass' mother in her little brown imitation brick house at the top of the Wood Street hill.

When they got to Hackley, they sold the old truck, and when school dismissed for the summer, Cass began his daily practice of walking the half block to the school yard where as a youngster he had first mastered the art of baseball, and there he became obsessed with teaching the neighborhood boys the finer points of the game. In the afternoon he went to the Sepia Club and got drunk.

Josie and Cass' mother took in laundry, made dresses and mended clothes. They managed on their meager income, and Cass had enough money from his settlement to get drunk every afternoon.

CHAPTER FOUR

The Neighborhood

On the north side of Cass's house, a two-track road ran along the top edge of the valley, curling its way the entire mile eastward from Wood Street to Getty. Tractors, garbage trucks, pickups, boys on bicycles and pedestrians, even tramps looking for hand-outs during the depression, had worn a parallel pair of bumpy ruts into the rich soil behind Amity Street. North of the two-track a steep hill covered with trees, brush, sand burrs and milkweeds descended to the celery flats below. Every few hundred yards or so a service road angled down from the two-track to the celery fields. The ball field, the two-track, the hill and the cool, clear creek that splashed along the celery flats comprised our playground.

The two-track bordered the nether lands of Amity Street. Scaling backs of garages stood in sharp contrast to the neatly painted fronts that faced the street. A trash barrel smoldered perpetually behind VanDam's garage and overflowing garbage cans waited behind Kroeze's for the truck to come. The older Bytwork boys had left a broken-down, red Model T convertible to gather rust behind their garage. We called it a Tin Lizzie. Mr. Schuitema stored an old wheel-less Plymouth up on blocks behind his, a trophy of the great depression. The Rottman boys had nailed a bushel basket up on the back of their garage so they could play basketball, argue over rules, and chase errant rebounds down the hill beyond the two-track. Mrs. Bouma's pride was her compost heap that provided her tulips with the best growing power of any tulips on Amity Street, provided her husband with an abundance of fat fishing worms, and provided a host of buzzing flies their daily nourishment. And so on, past the back yards of Van Bruggen, Baker, Oosting, Bosch, Benton, Musch, Balkema and Witt.

It was the summer of 1944, my eleventh year. When we turned twelve, we were expected to spend our summer working full time in the celery farms. That was the Dutch way. The only boys exempt from that labor were those who played for Cass in the morning or those who had better jobs. So, my eleventh summer was my last free one, and I had hoped it would be one to remember. It was.

Calvin was my best friend. He had moved to Hackley from Canada four years earlier when his father, Dominie Johannes VandeBruin, accepted the call to be the dominie of the Ambrosia Avenue Church. Calvin and I did everything together. We went to the

The Neighborhood

Dutch Christian School together. We went to Sunday school and catechism together. Every other Sunday we ate dinner at each other's house. When we weren't in school, we would race our bikes along the dusty two-track, all the way from Wood to Getty. If it was hot, we would go down to the flats and splash naked in the creek that ran along the edge of the celery fields. At one point, just before the creek emerged from the marsh, it widened and deepened into the finest swimming hole anyone could imagine. The older boys would go for a swim after a hot day in the celery fields. In the winter we rode our sleds, tearing down the service roads and flying over the wooden bridge out on to the frozen fields. If it was icy enough we could slide all the way across the field.

Donny and Chuckie Eldersveld lived next door to me. Donny was a good ball player and was in the ninth grade, but Chuckie was only in the fifth. He tagged along with us because there were no other fifth graders in the neighborhood. Since he was younger, he always sucked up to us and would do most anything we asked. Once he stole some of his dad's cigarettes and we went down into the woods below the two-track to smoke them. Chuckie and Calvin got sick, but I didn't.

If you went south out of my house, turned left at VanDam's corner and went east on Amity Street to just past the Baker's, you would come to the house of Hickey Bishop. A year or two after Calvin moved to Hackley, Hickey moved into Widow Oosting's old house.

Mrs. Oosting's husband had died a several years before that. He was a huckster who rode around town in a horse drawn wagon, hollering, "tomatoes, potatoes, squash, lettuce, kale," or any produce that happened to be in season. I don't know what his real name was, but the Dutch people had nick named him Tipper because he sat on the bench of his wagon sipping whiskey as he made his rounds.

Early every morning Tipper Oosting started at the farmers' produce market where he bought his fruit and vegetables, stopped next at Petrone's grocery and liquor store for a pint, and began his trip through the streets of Hackley. He was a fixture. He never went to church, but his wife went faithfully every Sunday.

One day when he was drunk he wandered out into the street and got run over by a car.

A few years after Tipper Oosting was killed, his wife, Ella, died too, and her nephew, Hickey Bishop, moved into their house. The Dutch people laughingly nicknamed him Hickey because he too drank whiskey. Carried on the family tradition, I guess. No one except Dominie VandeBruin took his drinking very seriously. It gave the town something to joke about.

But before you got to Hickey Bishop's house, you had to pass a row of typically nice, two story Dutch homes, all neatly painted, lawns trimmed, shrubbery poodled and gardens decorated with shapely patches of colorful tulips in the spring and other flowers during the rest of the summer.

Then, at the S curve the architecture abruptly changed. Hickey's house was a single story bungalow made of drab brown imitation brick shingles, as was the home of his neighbor, little Albert Bosch, the ragman. The ruder neighbors called their houses tarpaper shacks. A wild growth of shrubbery guarded the fronts of both humble homes.

Next to Albert lived the Bentons on the far end of the S curve. They had a big old two story dark house with a barn out back in which they boarded horses for Sanitary Dairy and the Hackley Police Department. Mr. Benton also had horses that adults and big kids could ride for a small fee. Beyond Benton's, the neat row of Dutch houses resumed and continued all the way to Getty Street.

The Bentons didn't fit into the neighborhood. They weren't Dutch, they didn't go to church, and they didn't raise tulips or keep their house neatly painted or their front lawn and shrubs neatly trimmed. And their daughter, Audrey, went to the public school rather than our Christian School. Mr. Benton was a short, wiry, strong man who could lift heavy things and master powerful horses. We never knew if he did anything for a living except board horses and run the Veterans' Association Youth League.

But everyone knew that when he went to Hackley High School he was an excellent athlete and an all-state infielder who did a short stint in the minor leagues and knew Cass White real well. He was the only adult in the neighborhood who had anything to do with Cass.

Beside the garages and Benton's barn, there were no buildings behind that row of houses on the north side of Amity Street, just the two-track that serviced the celery farms and the green houses below. Since it started at Getty and came out just north of Cass White's house on Wood Street, you could walk on the path from Cass's place to the backside of Hickey's and Albert's without being noticed. When Calvin and I played along the path, we climbed mulberry trees, fired at rabbits with our slingshots, killed snakes with sticks or with the heels of our shoes, or lay in the tall grass of the embankment spying on our neighbors.

Once we watched Audrey Benton take a sunbath naked on the roof of her back porch, below her bedroom window. Though we went back again many times, we only saw her that once. She was in the eighth grade. We were only in the sixth, and she fascinated us because she was beginning to develop. We fantasized about her a lot and got ticks from lying in the tall grass hoping to see her naked just one more time.

CHAPTER FIVE

Hickey

Hickey was a different kind of drunk than Cass. Whereas Cass got drunk every afternoon and woke up sober every morning, Hickey got drunk every now and then and stayed drunk for several days, sometimes a week or more.

We attended catechism every Saturday and learned our Heidelberg under the tutelage of Dominie VandeBruin, Calvin's father. He also had practical advice for us. "Stay as far as you can from Hickey Bishop's house," the Dominie warned. "If you have to pass that way, cross to the opposite side of the street. That old drunkard is possessed by the evil spirits that come from the bottle, and if you get too close, they may come and enter you like those evil spirits came out of Legion and entered the pigs in Jesus' day. Drunkenness is catching, you know, and you don't want to become drunks like him."

Dominie VandeBruin preached to us a lot about strong drink. "It is the very embodiment of evil. It is the thing that robs a man of his senses and opens the door of his heart to let Satan in." He often used Cass and Hickey as his prime examples when he preached against the evils of drink. He did allow, however, that a Christian home was permitted to keep one bottle of whiskey in the upper cupboard to be used solely for medicinal purposes and to make a batch of Boeren Jongens to celebrate New Years.

My parents kept a bottle of medicinal whiskey that my mother never touched but that my dad sipped occasionally at night to ward off insomnia and aching muscles. Sometimes when we children had ailments such as a cold or sore throat, my dad would add a few drops of whiskey to a spoonful of sugar and serve it to us. He called it a whiskey sling. I don't know if it did any good or not, but it tasted terrible. In later years I've declared that it ruined both the whiskey and the sugar.

As youngsters we had no fear of Hickey. He was gangly, paunchy and awkward, so we knew we could outrun him if he ever got nasty with us, but he never did. Rather, he was quite kind. Sometimes when we were bored, which was frequently, we would lay our bikes beside the two-track and approach Hickey's place from the rear. Though he never ventured out his front door and never had any interaction with his Dutch neighbors, he secretly welcomed us youngsters into his back yard, but warned us never to tell our parents that we had visited him.

Being kids, we were happy to keep our covert visits with him secret. We enjoyed pretending to be spies and keeping confidential information close to our chests. It was like being an agent for the FBI. My parents never said much about Hickey, except that he was a drunk, but since Calvin's folks had made it clear that we were to keep away from him, our secret relationship with him was more than just fun. It was intrigue of the highest order and required each of us to have complete trust in the other.

We learned, by lying quietly in the tall grass just below the two-track, that Queen Anne came down the path to Hickey's every afternoon except Sunday carrying a picnic basket on her arm. We surmised that she came to cook and clean and do his laundry because when she was there we could smell meat cooking in his house and we would watch as she hung clothes out on the line. And we knew she left late in the afternoon. But we kept all that a secret too.

"How's Dominie VandeBruin?" Hickey often asked us when we stopped to visit him. We had told him that Calvin was the dominie's son and that we both went to his church. He was very pleased to know that. In fact, that bit of knowledge made him glow, and we could never understand why. When we told him that the dominie was fine, he always urged us to heed his words.

"Dominie VandeBruin is a good man, a true man of God. Learn your catechism well from him and study the scriptures. Grace is free for the elect, my dear boys, but you must apply yourself to the study of the Word in order to show yourself approved to the

Lord. Maybe someday you can be dominies like him, or maybe even professors in the seminary."

When he was sober he seemed bright enough to be a professor himself, a fact that left us baffled. So when he was drunk we laughingly called him Professor Hickey, behind his back, of course. In his presence we always called him sir.

When we first met him, he was plump and ungainly, and every time we saw him he appeared to be getting fatter. He seemed obsessed by food and always seemed to be eating, even between meals. When we last visited him, he was so fat he couldn't stand for long, and he struggled up the three steps to the big stuffed chair next to the screen door on his back porch. He would sit and fold his hands over his stomach, taking a long time to catch his breath after the climb up the three steps. Through the screen door we could see an old round dining table surrounded by three sturdy chairs. A single light bulb hung from a ceiling cord that was tied in a loop knot. The table was clean of dishes, but the odors of good cooking always seemed to seep through the doorway.

When he had breath again, he usually urged us to be good boys, to be attentive in church, and to study our catechism. "Especially be nice to Mr. Bosch. Don't harass him or tease him. He is a good man and he works very hard for what he has."

"Is Albert Bosch rich?" we would ask, having heard the rumor that somewhere on his junk filled lot he had hidden millions of dollars.

"In some ways he is very wealthy," Hickey would answer, "but in others he is very poor." His evasive answer did nothing to clear up the mystery. "But he is a very good man. A God-fearing man. One of the few pure servants of the Lord left on the face of this earth." After brief conversation, he usually asked us to run along, but declared that he would be happy to have our company again another day. Then he would close his eyes, push his spectacles back up to the bridge of his nose, and soon he would be snoring in his big chair on the back porch.

Hickey took a liking to me, though I could never understand why. I was no different than the other boys, but for some reason he singled me out and complimented me often. Sometimes, after we got to know him, I would visit him by myself. He liked that. We sometimes sat and talked for quite a while. "You are a bright boy, Christian," he would say, then pat me on the head and muss my hair. "Do you like to read?" he asked one day when we were sitting together on the grass embankment, looking down onto the celery flats.

"Yes, sir, I love reading," I answered.

"What do you read?" he asked.

"I like the Rover Boys and the Sugar Creek Gang books," I replied. "I like stories about boys. I like Horatio Alger's books."

"Good, good," he would respond, "Horatio Alger is a fine author. Very moral. Do you read Christian literature?"

"Yes sir, I read my Sunday school paper and I read the children's section in *The Clarion*. That is our church paper. We get it every week."

"Oh yes, I know it well. I read it too," he said as he smiled at me. "Do you study the children's lesson and answer the questions?"

"Yes, my mother always quizzes me on the questions," I said. His eyes glowed as though we had established a bond.

"And do you read the book, **Manna**?"

"Yes, dad reads it every day at supper, and when I made profession the church gave me a copy. I like it a lot."

The glow in his eye turned moist. After a long pause he asked, "What are you going to be when you grow up?"

"I think I'd like to write books," I responded, "books about boys."

"That is a noble profession, if you write decent books, that is," he said. "Write Christian literature. If you want to become a writer, mind your elders and do good work, especially in school. Be sure you get an education, and use your gifts for the Lord. He is the giver of all good and perfect gifts and will hold us accountable for our use of them, as he did in the parable of the talents. Will you write under your own name?"

"No," I answered, "I've already decided that I should use a pen name, like Mark Twain did."

"And have you decided what name would you use?"

"Christian Weaver, I think."

"Christian Weaver," he said thoughtfully, "what an appropriate name for a writer who weaves godly fictional homilies for boys."

"That's what I thought," I answered.

"Be sure you live your life on the straight and narrow, Christian. Look at those neat rows in the fields below. That is how your life should be. Neat and orderly, crisp and clean, like the celery. Once you stray from the straight and narrow, there may be no way back. Remember that, if you remember nothing else. But maintain your humility, son, be sure to maintain your humility. God doesn't like the proud." He didn't seem nearly as evil as Dominie VandeBruin made him out to be.

A big old sugar maple grew between Hickey's and Albert's, and was surrounded by brambles that clogged the space between their two houses. There might have been a fence connecting their houses right through the middle of the shrubs, I don't know. If there was, you couldn't see it. On the other side, a tall wooden fence ran the full distance from the back corner of Hickey's house all the way to Baker's garage, either to keep him in or the Baker boys out, I don't know. So you couldn't get to the sidewalk from Hickey's back yard. A driveway between Albert's and Benton's was the only access from the street, and Mr. Benton kept a big saw horse across the front of it to discourage people from coming in.

Often when Hickey fell asleep, instead of going back to our bikes sometimes we would sneak over to

Albert's place and scavenge among the rows of salvage neatly arranged in his back yard. Just on his side of the two-track he had a row of old stoves. Next was a row of old wash machines, then a row of old iceboxes, and then a row of old bald tires. Between the tires and the back of his house were neat piles of everything from old kitchen utensils to old automobile parts. Everything was old. Though we scoured the ovens, the wash machines and the iceboxes for his reputed cache of money, we never found a cent. He was either really poor or he had hidden his money very well.

CHAPTER SIX

Albert

Albert Bosch was a pathetic little gnome of a man who suffered merciless torment at the hands of the Hackley boys, including me. His pushcart was a brilliant green wooden box with two large, red wheels with metal rims that grated on the pavement as he scurried through the neighborhoods. His known benefactors were the firemen at Number Two Station on Wood Street who painted his cart annually and outfitted it with red reflectors to keep him from being hit by a car as he pushed his way back up Getty Street hill at dusk on his way home from the Rag & Metal. They also kept him in kerosene during the winter. Mr. Benton looked after him somewhat and made sure his kerosene heater worked properly when winter came.

The frugal Dutch, finding it more important to exercise good stewardship than to practice charity to the poor, found it practical to accept Albert's meager offering of small coins in exchange for their old tires, stacks of papers, bent wheels, old hubcaps, and any other bit of trash that they couldn't pay the garbage men to haul away. And when they had no other option, they would drop off their old stoves, wash machines and iceboxes in the driveway beside his house, and Mr. Benton, his neighbor, would wrestle them to the deepest part of Albert's back yard. Albert always appreciated any donation, whether he could transport it and sell it or not.

Albert was a scrawny five feet tall, not much taller than we were. His left foot toed inward and he always placed it in front of himself as he lowered his left shoulder, wrapped his arm around the U shaped handle, and muscled the cart from house to house. His left arm was deformed and his twisted hand jutted out at a right angle from his wrist. Often we followed him, laughing and imitating his grotesque walk. His hair was oily, dark and straight, awkwardly cut and never properly combed. His left eye was permanently closed, if he had any eye there at all. His right eye watered copiously, and he squinted as though it irritated him. He suffered a speech impediment, articulating with difficulty from the right side of his mouth while the left side seemed to be glued shut.

He always went about his business with resolute detachment. Pausing obediently when we asked him to show us his money, he would patiently open his little snap purse, hold it up close to his one good eye, and carefully count his coins by moving them around inside the purse with a finger that couldn't bend. While one of us distracted him, another would snatch an old bent hubcap from his wagon and offer it to him for sale.

"How much will you give me for this nice hubcap, Albert?"

He would take it in his gnarled hands, hold it close to his face and look it over carefully. "A penny," he would answer. Then we would sell him his own hubcap and ride off with his penny to buy ourselves a package of peanut butter Kits.

Another way we riled him over and over was to impede his wagon with our bikes, and when he tried to circumvent us, pretend to get our foot run over by one of his steel wheels. We would roll on the ground, feigning injury, and giggling as Albert became frantic and wrung his hands in guilt and sympathy. When we had had our pleasure, we simply rode off laughing. That streak of meanness has haunted me all the rest of my life.

At the end of each day his destination was the Rag & Metal, a sprawling junkyard at the northeast corner of town. About a half mile beyond the S curve, Amity Street ran into Getty. From that corner, Getty descended on a long slope northward down to the celery flats, crossed the flats, then ascended to an industrial area that included, among other enterprises, The Hackley Motor Works, the Rag & Metal, Petrone's Grocery and Liquor Store. It was a long way to walk, much less push a wagon loaded with trash.

As he descended, he had to hook his arm around the handle of his cart and lean back into the hill to keep the cart from running away. As he ascended the other side, he had to lean into the cart, and if he had an especially heavy load he had to brace himself with each step to keep the cart from rolling back on him. Mr. Amsterdam at the Rag & Metal usually paid Albert a pittance for the junk he had spent the day collecting, but sometimes told him he was sorry but there was no room for some large, worthless item he brought in that day.

When the war started, Mr. Amsterdam paid him well for old tires, but soon the people caught on and brought their own worn out tires to the Rag & Metal for salvage. After he had sold all he could sell to Mr. Amsterdam, Albert would return laboriously the way he had come and, with Mr. Benton's help, unload his leftovers in the neat rows and piles behind his house. Thus his collection of relics.

CHAPTER SEVEN

Professor Bisschop

Just how Hickey Bishop came to dwell among us is a fascinating story that requires us to return to his younger days, long before he ever came to Hackley.

Professor Pieter Bisschop, a tall, gangly scholar with a slightly paunched stomach that was beginning to testify to his love of good food, was more than teacher and academic advisor to seminarian Johannes VandeBruin. He was his mentor. Recognizing in him a spark of commitment, devotion and energy a cut above the others, he separated him out for special tutoring.

"Johannes," he would say, thoughtfully pushing his spectacles up to the bridge of his nose, "our faith is being put at risk daily by self-serving men who challenge the wisdom of John Calvin, especially when it comes to the necessity of sanctified living. Focus your ministry on living as our Savior would have us live.

Study his teachings, especially his parables. There's great wisdom in the parables."

"Yes, professor," Johannes would answer, "every day in every class I see my professors and classmates questioning the relationship between grace and works, focusing on our election and discounting the merits of righteous living."

"They do that to justify their own misbehavior," the professor would respond, "thinking that they can be carnal with impunity. They forget that faith without works is vain and forget that they have to work to make their election sure. They want to think that their being predestined for glory allows them great latitude of conduct."

"My eternal mission will be to serve my flock as Calvin served his in Geneva," Johannes would avow, "being a model of purity for them and urging them to live in accordance with the laws of scripture and the rules of the church."

"Yes, Johannes," he would say, "we are soldiers in the Church militant, and we are shepherds to our flocks. And just as David used his weapons to ward off the wild animals that threatened his sheep, we must use the sword of the Spirit to defend the members of our congregations from the wiles of the devil."

"Yes sir," Johannes would answer, quoting scripture, "the devil is like a roaring lion seeking whom he may devour."

"And as Martin Luther observed," proclaimed the professor, "he is our ancient foe who seeks to work us woe. His craft and power are great, and he's armed with cruel hate. Sing those words over and over again, Johannes."

"And he's bound to strike us when we least expect," Johannes would respond, "as he struck our first parents there in paradise."

"He will strike us where we are most vulnerable, and he will strike where he can do the most damage. He knows he is destined to the eternal flames of hell and he wants more than anything to take us with him."

"So we must engender in our flocks the passion to live righteously, to understand Satan's ways, and to be prepared to do battle against the forces of evil."

"But gently, Johannes, gently. And humbly. Not with pride or superiority. Men are by nature weak, you know, and given to all sorts of depravity. I've even heard that some of our colleagues are beginning to imbibe. They forget that as dominies they are the princes of the church and that the Wisdom of Solomon forbids them to take strong drink. Dominies must demonstrate abstinence and teach virtue. I've heard lately that some of our colleagues are advocating the title *Reverend* instead of *Dominie*. All of the respect with none of the responsibility of lordship."

"So we must be firm in our teaching and our righteousness, must we not?" Johannes would ask.

"Yes, firm, but not harsh, and above all, humble," his mentor would repeat as Johannes admiringly eyed the elegant bronze nameplate on the professor's desk which made known to all that the man sitting on the other side was *Pieter E. Bisschop, Doctor of Theol-*

ogy. It was a gift from his aunt Ella Oosting that he cherished and displayed proudly on his desk at the seminary, especially since he knew she could ill afford such a costly gift.

"We must live so the world may see our good works and glorify our Father in heaven," the professor frequently reminded all of his students, "that is scriptural, but we must never become pharisaical about it. We may not judge other sinners, judgment is God's business, so we must never usurp his throne by attempting to judge and punish sinners ourselves. And most importantly, we must never ignore the poor, the sick and the discomfited. We are to be their light and their salt."

At those words, the young seminarian winced but nodded in reluctant compliance, feeling that his professor had subtly found him guilty of trespassing into God's purview.

Professor Bisschop was younger than he appeared, having finished seminary less than a decade earlier and having earned his doctorate degree just three years before VandeBruin entered the seminary. While teaching in the seminary, Bisschop had authored a brilliant and very readable devotional entitled *Manna*. It was based on the Heidelberg Catechism and had not only become standard daily reading at most Dutch dinner tables, but almost overnight had been translated into Dutch, French and German and was becoming as well known throughout Canada and Europe as it was in America. Since it was of such caliber that one could read it over and over from year to year and always glean some new wisdom from it, it remained a staple of the faith and earned the professor substantial recognition as well as a perpetual income far above what he earned as an educator. Dutch churches across the continent and in the Old Country habitually gave a gift copy to every youngster who made profession of faith.

It was truly a masterpiece, an inspired piece of work that got him promoted to chairman of the theology department after only three years of teaching in the seminary. Over the course of a year of daily readings based on the Heidelberg Catechism, it explained how the sin committed by Adam and Eve plunged all of humanity into torment, detailed our deliverance from sin and misery purely by the grace of God, and challenged us to come apart from the world and live sanctified lives in gratitude for our deliverance. Johannes VandeBruin treasured the book as much as he idolized its author.

Professor Bisschop was also a gifted preacher, filling pulpits frequently in churches a short distance from the seminary. The Dutch of Hackley held him in high esteem, and on several Sundays he preached at the Ambrosia Avenue church when it had no dominie of its own. He made his Aunt Ella proud, though few of the congregation comprehended the relationship or remembered his visiting her when he was a child.

When Johannes VandeBruin graduated from the seminary he earned the title of Dominie and accepted a call to serve as pastor of a church in Canada where he based much of his preaching on the work of his idol, Professor Bisschop. Right after graduation he married Gertrude VanTil, and a year later, Calvin was born. Two years after that Calvin's little sister Gracie was born. When they moved to Hackley, they lived in the parsonage about three blocks south of me, right next to the big, white-pillared church on Ambrosia Avenue. Johannes and his mentor corresponded frequently for a short time after his graduation, then the unthinkable happened.

CHAPTER EIGHT

The Necessity of Pious Living

It had become the practice of a few of the liberal thinkers on the seminary faculty to gather with measured secrecy in the back room of Gerdes's Tavern on Franklin Street on Friday evening for debate and libation, filling the room with clouds of pipe and cigar smoke and the fumes of other diverse spirits as well as words. Bisschop, of course, would never attend such gatherings, deigning them satanic attempts to lead the elect astray, if that were possible.

But on a fateful Friday, one of his liberal colleagues who had recently come over from the Netherlands informed him that the topic for the evening was to be the "necessity of pious living," and that some powerful tongues were to argue the side of Christian liberty. Fearing that such debate had the potential of tainting the whole body of Christ, Bisschop decided to sit in on the discussion and do all he could to hold his beloved flock of seminarians to the standards set by the founders of the faith.

After hours of lively, and sometimes arduous debate, the gentle but firm professor got thirsty, and in a thoughtless moment almost by necessity tasted whiskey for the first time in his life. The colleague sitting next to him poured him a shot glass full, and Pieter sipped it with pursed lips and a watery squint. At first it was intriguingly bitter and tingly on his dry tongue, then he swallowed, and the whiskey slid down, burning his throat and stomach with a forbidden ecstasy, and as he sipped, it soon began to clear his hoarse throat and calm his harrowed mind. He spoke on and on, convinced now that the whiskey made him comfortable, more eloquent, more lucid and spry of tongue. So as he debated he drank on, and shortly after midnight they carried him to his small apartment over Fiorelli's Grocery Store on Franklin Street, two blocks up from Gerdes's Tavern, dead drunk.

He stayed drunk for more than a week on the whiskey delivered to him by his new friends, and eating roast beef sandwiches and home made chocolate cupcakes brought in by Mrs. Fiorelli, wife of the grocery store proprietor who lived in the adjacent apartment.

His superiors believed that he had the flu, and those who knew the truth guarded it jealously. During his week of stupor, a few close companions took turns staying with him, and he finally sobered up, but was too ashamed to show his face at the seminary again. His friends gathered his belongings from his office and he wrote a brief letter of resignation, apologizing for his sudden departure and asserting that he had been urgently called to pursue the Lord's interests elsewhere. Given the esteem in which he was held, no one questioned his actions.

Dominie VandeBruin, believing he had returned to the Old Country, lost all track of him, but he faithfully read and preached from his treasured devotional, *Manna*. And Professor Bisschop remained forever his idol.

And so Professor Pieter Bisschop moved into the fully furnished bungalow on Amity Street that his aunt, the Widow Oosting, had owned. He opened an account and ordered his publisher to deposit the ever growing royalties from his devotional directly to the bank. Then he began his mostly solitary and secret life, reading, writing, and visiting almost exclusively with very limited company that included, of course, us boys.

He settled into his Aunt Ella's humble little bungalow next to Albert Bosch's humble little bungalow with his cartons of books and an endless supply of writing pads, though he never intended to publish anything ever again. He loved to read and he loved to write, and he had a habit of keeping a meticulous record of his daily activities, his memories and conversations, as though order were among life's higher virtues. He wrote almost daily on pads of yellow paper, dated his writings, and when he had filled a pad he carefully packed it into one of the many beer cartons in which Albert brought home his groceries from Petrone's.

When a carton was full, he taped it shut with packing tape and carried it to Albert's shed for storage. He always put mothballs inside the cartons to keep mice away. In later years I came to possess his cartons of notes, which explains why I am privy to things in his life beyond what I have been able to observe first hand, including the mystery of how he came to live there.

His notes were orderly and well written. He bemoaned the fact that he had become an exile from the academic world, but was, in a way, grateful for his exile because it opened up for him new doors of insight and thought, especially about the notion of sanctified living. He had become aware not only of the truth that one might live a righteous life only by the grace of God, but also that sanctification might not really be what he thought it to have been.

The yellow pads became his both diary and his confessional. He kept careful record of his sins, to the best of his sometimes shaky recollection.

Prior to his plunge into drunkenness, he held firmly to the idea that grateful Christians had to separate themselves from the world and deny themselves the pleasure of doing all of those things that might offend God. That was the doctrine he preached in the seminary, the doctrine Dominie VandeBruin took to the pulpit, and the doctrine the Dutch of Hackley lived by. But truth seen through the back window of a tarpaper shack isn't the same color as the truth seen through the beveled glass window of a third floor seminary office. And the professor, now known simply as Hickey, was beginning to see the difference. The "thou shalt nots" of theological academia were being replaced by "thou shalts," and he began to understand the reality of the fact that being his brother's keeper went far beyond keeping his saintly brother from falling into sin. The parable of the Good Samaritan became his favorite of Christ's teachings.

His widowed aunt, Ella Oosting, I learned from his notes, died childless just months before his sudden departure from the seminary. Since he was her next of kin, he was heir to the property. He had visited her there several times in the summer when he was a child and had some recollection of the neighborhood.

A friend from the seminary who owned a Chevy coupe, Daniel Meeter, drove the unfrocked professor to Hackley, towing a small trailer containing a trunk of clothing, towels and bed linens, and several cartons full of canned food, note pads, books, personal belongings, a few spare copies of *Manna*, and, of course, a fifth of whiskey that might be useful in the future. Before they arrived at the house, they stopped at the bank where he opened his accounts and arranged for the deposit of his royalty checks directly from the publishing company. He Anglicized his surname to Bishop, a practice adopted by the more liberal Dutch but distained by old order folks, and, in the hope of maintaining anonymity, registered his given name at the post office and bank as P. Edward Bishop. They brought the trunk and boxes in through the front door, and when he closed it to let Daniel out, he bolted it, never to open it again.

CHAPTER NINE

Josie LaFarge

A few days after he moved in, Hickey remembered that he could take a walk along the two-track out back and not be seen by any of his neighbors. He had become a determined recluse, preferring to find only minimal and very private company and limiting his travels to the two-track between Wood and Getty. As he wandered westward one day looking down through the trees to the celery flats, he was surprised to find himself suddenly at Wood Street, at the end of the two-track, and at the edge of the Negro Section. He paused in the shadows of the tall shrubs along the crest of the hill and witnessed Cass White leaving from the front door of his house for his daily walk to the Sepia Club. Queen Anne came out to the front steps in her housecoat and kissed him goodbye. Hickey stood in stunned silence, feeling more like a voyeur than an honest pedestrian. Instead of reentering the front door of her house, Queen Anne walked around the side, toward Hickey and toward the back porch. When she saw him she stopped and instinctively drew her housecoat tightly around her. They looked at each other for a moment. She spoke first.

"Who might you be?"

He paused, as if trying to remember his name. "I'm, ah, Edward Bishop," he answered, haltingly, unused to such company and unused to being at a loss for words. To bolster his anonymity he paused to make sure he used only his middle name. "I live alone a few houses back," he said as he pointed eastward. "I'm sorry to have intruded into your privacy."

"I be Josie Anne LaFarge," she offered and, seemingly desperate to share her plight with someone, began to talk freely. "Casien White be my man. He take care of me. No, I guess we take care of one 'nother." Without a trace of reticence she stepped closer to him, scrutinizing him from head to toe. "Casien was a ball player, a good one, they said he was the naturalest player that ever was. But he can't play no more. He got hurt in the head and don't see and don't think so good no more. In the summer he teach ball to the young boys. And he just drink ever day to forget his misery. He has to."

Hickey was taken back by her outpouring of personal matters to a complete stranger, but welcoming the opportunity for conversation he answered, "I can understand that. At times I have bitter distress myself."

"But he be a good man. He teach his boys. He take care of me. I be all he got since his mama die." Then a tear came to her eye. She tingled for a moment, feeling she was offering too much information, but something inside her that she didn't understand compelled her to continue. "But now we be broke. Casien settlement done run out. I don't know what we do. Mr. Denhof come tomorrow for the rent, and that is almost our last money. I guess I take to 'ho'in'. He get his head busted for me, so it be okay if I be a 'ho for him. Not for nobody else. You got a woman?"

Hickey shuddered at the word whore. He had read it in the King James Bible and had heard it used by men, but never by a woman, and he had never met a woman who spoke so candidly. She seemed bright, enchanting and good, though illiterate. He was fearfully intrigued and suddenly comprehended that she was speaking to him out of some sense of panic and trepidation, hoping that some remedy might come from it and disaster be averted.

"No!" he exclaimed, "you must maintain your marital purity," he responded instinctively. "Harlotry is no solution for poverty."

She took a step back and looked downward.

Then, in a moment of inspiration he asked, "Are you qualified for domestic service?"

"What?"

"Can you clean and cook and sew and do laundry?"

"Oh yes, I be a good maid, but nobody around here hire a maid."

"What are your financial requirements?"

"What?"

"How much money do you need each month to sustain... ah to live on...you and, uh, your Casien?" he asked, beginning to sense in his spirit what the true character of pious living might be, of living with an open hand, an open heart and an open mind.

"The rent done went up to twenty a month and Casien need a dollar ever day to go downtown. Then they's groceries and the electric, and kerosene, and ice and stuff. You want some coffee?" She smiled at him, stepping up to the porch. Fascinated, he accepted her invitation, climbed the steps to the porch, and took the chair across from her at the table.

Hickey did a quick calculation while she poured his coffee. "If I were to pay you, say, sixty a month plus some groceries, would you come to my house for a few hours each day and cook for me, clean and do my laundry? Would that eliminate your need to, ah, prostitute yourself?"

"Oh, if I had that kind of job I wouldn't have to go 'ho'in'."

"What may I call you?" he asked, leaning forward and noticing that her eyes were blue.

"Josie," she responded, "that be my name."

"Josie," he murmured.

As she poured him a second cup, her housecoat fell open and revealed a bit of her cleavage. She saw him looking and closed the opening at her neck. They talked over the last of the coffee and settled on the arrangement Hickey had offered.

"I live just east of here," he explained, "between the Bakers and Mr. Bosch."

"I walk in the alley sometime. I know your house," she responded, "'twix the Dutch peoples and the junk man."

"That's my house. When you come, be sure to stay back here on the two-track, and be sure you aren't seen. I don't want my neighbors to know I have employed a maid. Can you start today?"

"I be there soon as I fix up here," she said with a tone of relief.

Then he went back home. "How providential, how providential...," he kept muttering to himself as he strolled back on the two-track. An hour later she appeared at his back door, neatly attired in a black dress and white apron, but incredulous that he lived in such a modest house and wanted a maid.

"You sure you can pay me Mr. Bishop?" she asked.

"Josie, I've chosen to live as a penitent. The Lord has brought me down from high places and has called me to live humbly and alone. This little house is my penitentiary. Here is your first month's pay in advance," he said, handing her three twenties. "I'm giving this to you in good faith, fully expecting that you will honor your pledge to work for me and remain faithful to your husband."

Thus it came to pass that Josie LaFarge became Hickey's cook and housekeeper. Every noon after Cass left for the Sepia, she donned her black dress and white apron and walked the two-track to Hickey's, cooked him a good meal with an abundance of leftovers, cleaned his house, did his laundry, and went home with a basket of food sufficient to feed herself and Cass the next day.

CHAPTER TEN

Neighbors

A week after he employed Josie, Hickey went next door to visit Albert. He had seen him wheel his cart around to the rear of his house at the end of the day and park it in the little wooden shed that stood right next to Mr. Benton's barn. He remembered the little ragman from his childhood as a kindly, friendly fellow, so, desperately in need of some sort of honest male intellectual comradeship, he walked over into Albert's back yard and introduced himself.

"Hello, I'm Edward Bishop," he said, offering his hand to the shriveled little man whose appearance the years seemed not to have changed in the least. To Hickey he looked old thirty years ago, and still looked as old today.

"Alber' Bosch," he replied, extending his hand, but withdrawing it again and looking toward the ground.

"Mr. Bosch, I've just recently moved in next door, and I'd like us to be good neighbors. Would you do me the honor of coming to my house for supper? I have some nice beef roast still warm in the pot. I would appreciate your company."

"That would be nice," Albert responded. "I used to eat with the Widow Oosting on Sunday when she come home from church." He paused. "But she died."

"Yes, I know," Hickey explained. "The Widow Oosting was my aunt. She never had any children so, my being her sole survivor, I inherited her place. I live here now and I'm happy to have you as my neighbor."

"She had a little nep'yew who come to visit sometime in the summer. I remember him. Petey he was. A good little boy. He was very bright. Growed up and preached here in the 'Brosia church."

"Yes, yes, I remember little Petey," Hickey reminisced. "He was a good little boy." The connection and the irony being lost on Albert, Hickey explained that he was Petey, all grown up.

"I became a professor of theology at the seminary, Mr. Bosch, but I suffered some misfortune there and have decided to spend my life here in seclusion. But I'd appreciate that being our little secret, agreed? I'm plain Edward Bishop now."

Albert nodded in assent, honored to be privy to a secret of such magnitude.

Having already asked Josie about him, in addition to what he remembered of the past, Hickey knew quite a bit about Albert, including the fact that he made regular rounds through the neighborhoods, daily trips to the Rag & Metal and that neighborhood boys pestered him wherever he went. He also knew that Albert's meals consisted mostly of a noon lunch he got through the generosity of the Soldiers of the Cross, a mission on the dilapidated edge of downtown. They also usually gave him a small sack of leftovers that served as his breakfast and supper.

Albert was only too eager to sit down to a meal of roast beef, potatoes, and green beans. He ate without speaking, and though his table manners were primitive, Hickey did not look down upon him or demonstrate superiority. He was truly on a mission to serve his Lord humbly, fully confident that as one of God's elect, he was serving a divine purpose despite the thorn in his flesh that he was managing to keep, at least for the moment, under control.

"Mr. Bosch, I think we can help each other," Hickey said after Albert had finished eating. "I don't get out at all, but I stay here and work at my table every day, reading and writing. My housekeeper did my grocery shopping this week at Doorn's grocery, but it would not be convenient for her to continue to do that. I understand that you pass by Petrone's Market every day. Is that right?"

"That's right, Mr. Bishop," Albert stammered.

"Mr. Bosch, I would be grateful if you would be so kind as to stop at Petrone's once or twice a week and obtain for me my list of groceries. I'll give you an envelope containing a shopping list and a check, and I would like you to transport the groceries and return my change, which may, at times, be a substantial sum since it is my only source of cash. Then, from time to time, upon request, I would like you to secure for me a bottle or two of whiskey."

Since he never drank anything stronger than coffee, Albert grimaced at the thought of purchasing whiskey, but Hickey continued. "I'm making the necessary arrangements by mail. I'll give you a note to pass on to the store keeper with a check in an envelope, and he will put the whiskey in your wagon and cover it so no one will see it. If you do those things for me, I'll see that you get a good meal every night when you get home, and I'll see to it that any other need you may have is supplied."

It was the guarantee of a regular supper that won Albert over, and in short order he agreed. "One more thing, Mr. Bosch, do you go to church?"

"No, I ain't got no church clothes," Albert answered. "Domie Vannerbine told all the people they was suppose to wear church clothes. We have to put our best foot forward for the Lord. But all I got is overalls and work shirts."

"We'll see to the matter of clothing. Once we get you properly attired, I'd like you to go to church on Sunday, listen carefully, and after services come to my house for dinner, bring me the church bulletin and discuss with me Dominie VandeBruin's message. Would you be so kind as to do that?"

Without hesitation, Albert nodded in agreement.

"And do you read, Mr. Bosch?"

"Oh yes, I read the Bible every morning with my coffee and toast. Right now I'm in King Sollyman's Proverbs. Mr. Benton brings me the *Cromical* every night after he's done with it so I get the news."

"I'd like to give you a copy of my book. It's named *Manna*. It contains daily readings based on the Heidelberg Catechism. It would serve you well as your morning devotions, your daily bread, so to speak. But again, I'd be grateful if you kept my authorship of the book our secret." Hickey got up from the table and from his bedroom brought Albert a beautiful, leather bound copy of his book. Albert took the book, gratefully clutched it to his chest, thanked Hickey profusely, and went home for the night.

The next morning he read the first devotion, carefully placed *Manna* in the drawer next to his Bible, and went out and began his rounds, comforted and grateful that the blood of Jesus had "fully satisfied for all his sins."

CHAPTER ELEVEN

A Sanctified Suit

"Good afternoon, Josie," Hickey greeted her when she knocked on his back door one day. "How are your tailoring skills?"

"My what?"

"Do you sew, altar clothing and the like?"

"Yes, I sew good. You want me to let out your britches? I'm going to have to if you keep eatin' my cookin' like you do."

"Well, we'll tend to that if the necessity arises," he responded without a smile. "Mr. Bosch needs a suit for church. I imagine he's rather difficult to fit, and we prefer to avoid the local clothiers. Have you any thoughts?"

"You got a fine suit hangin' in your closet. I see it when I put up you clothes. It soon ain't gon' fit you no mo', I can fix that for Mr. Albert."

"No, Josie, I'm saving that suit."

"Is you goin' to church with Mr. Albert?"

"No, Josie. The church would not accept me in my sinful condition."

"Is you goin' to hell, Mr. Edward?"

"That is a difficult question for me to answer, Josie. Some months ago I was sure of my election and working to preserve that assurance. Now I have a maze of contradictions to work through. It is a struggle. I feel as though I am one of the elect, but I am alienated from the body. Perhaps the Lord is using me in another way. His ways are inscrutable, you know."

"So you be savin' that suit for comin' back to the church?"

"If not for that, for a respectable burial, Josie. No matter what my life is like, I hope to have a respectable burial. Someday I must make preparations."

"Well, I think you look real good in that funeral suit, Mr. Edward. Real good, if'n they can stuff you in it."

"Back to business," he changed the subject. "Do you have any ideas for a suit for Mr. Bosch?"

She thought for a moment. "Casien do have an old suit that he don't wear no more. I might could take it up, if I had a sewin' machine. We sole ours to the ragman, to Mr. Albert, two year ago when the kerosene heater broke and we need a new one."

"I wonder if Mr. Bosch still might have that machine. We shall ask."

Then after a pause, Josie looked up, and with a smile on her lips and a twinkle in her eye said, "But it do be a sanctified suit, Mr. Edward. Do they 'low a sanctified suit in the white church?"

Failing to understand the humor of her comment he replied, "Sanctification only applies to the person, Josie, material things cannot be sanctified, only devoted. That is an error of the papists."

She looked at him blankly, "My Casien get sanctified in Memphis at the New Jerusalem Baptist Church. He carry on, singin', prophesyin' an' testifyin' like you never hear," she laughed. Then, becoming serious, "That was before he bust his head. He can't even think about Jesus no more. Jus' baseball and drinkin'. I go alone to the Zion Church where Reverend Jones be preachin'. "

"Does Casien drink because he can no longer play baseball?" He asked.

"That be the main reason," she replied, "but he also sad because the Color boys can't play on no real teams."

"Why can't the Colored boys play on teams?"

"They can't play on the White boys' teams and they can't get no sponsor. Ever team need a sponsor so they have shirts with numbers on the back. The hardware store sponsor the White boys who live around here. They have red shirts what tell the store on the front and numbers on the back. The grocery store over the hill sponsor a team, and so do the car man on Apple Street. But nobody sponsor the Color boys. That make Casien sad."

He looked down at his hands, flexing his fingers and feeling somewhat embarrassed by the situation. He furled his brow as though pondering a quandary but unable to resolve it. She saw that he was troubled, so she changed the subject. "This be the end of the leftovers, Mr. Edward. They be just enough stew left for you and Mr. Albert and me and Casien for today. Then everything be gone."

"Mr. Bosch has a list and will be shopping this afternoon," he said, grateful for the diversion. "Then we'll have enough for another week."

"Not if you keep eatin' like you do," she joked. "You gon' bust your britches, then I haffa fix 'em." This time he smiled slightly. "Mr. Edward," she said, "if you don't mind my sayin' so, you ain't very good at makin' up the lis. You forget 'portant stuff like salt an' bakin' powder. Flour ain't no good without bakin' powder. Can't make no biscuits with just flour and eggs," she laughed, "And we can't eat just roastin' beef, taters and green beans all the time. If'n I make the lis' I be makin' you some yummy good chocolate cake."

"Okay, Josie, you make out the list. I'll limit myself to what I can do competently, and allow you to do what you do competently. You formulate the shopping list."

While he sat at the table reading and writing, she stayed until late in afternoon, straightening up the place, cleaning, hanging up his clothes and cooking a pot of stew, using left over roast beef and vegetables. Then she went home.

Shortly after she left, Albert returned with a load of groceries, including fresh meat. "By the way, do you still have in your possession the sewing machine you bought from Miss Josie a few years ago."

"Oh yes, that's a nice machine. Pretty. I got it in the house. Mr. Benton helped me carry it in. It's just there to be pretty. I don't know how to use it."

"We must let Miss Josie use it to prepare your church suit."

Albert seemed excited by the idea of having a new suit of clothes. "Where do we get it"?

"Miss Josie will take care of that. You should be sure to be home early tomorrow afternoon for a fitting." Hickey dished out the stew and they ate in silence. Then Albert went home.

The next day Josie brought in a sack containing Cass's old suit that he didn't wear any more and an old white shirt and tie. Late in the afternoon they walked over to Albert's house, and a tear slid down Josie's cheek when she spied Mama's old treadle sewing machine in the corner.

When Albert got home she opened the bag, took out the clothes and held them up for Hickey and Albert to see. It was a charcoal black suit with thin white pin stripes and wide lapels with deep notches. Albert was delighted. He went to the bathroom to put it on and emerged moments later grinning broadly and holding the rolled up pants with hands that struggled to escape from the long coat sleeves. But both Hickey and Josie took the matter seriously. Albert stood on an old wooden box while Josie, mouth full of straight pins, ran her hands over Albert's body, tucking here and pinning there for what seemed hours until she had tailored the suit to her satisfaction. For the next week she spent an extra hour each day in Albert's house altering the garments. By the following Saturday it was finished, and Hickey paid Josie twenty dollars for the suit and the alterations.

It didn't look bad. The trouser legs were a little baggy, the shoulders too wide, and the tie a little sporty for a ragman, but all in all it didn't look bad. On Saturday night he bathed and shaved, and early Sunday morning Hickey helped him comb his hair. By nine o'clock the dapper Albert Bosch began his walk to church, carrying his Bible.

He slipped into the back row, hoping no one would notice. Being horribly myopic, he didn't know if the other worshippers were looking at him or not, but in his new suit he didn't feel out of place. No one sat beside him. He held the hymnbook close to his good eye and did the best he could to follow along. He remembered most of the old songs, and he surprised himself by still being able to recite most of the Apostle's Creed. He listened intently to the long prayer and the sermon, and afterward hurried home for Sunday dinner and conversation with Mr. Bishop.

He changed into his old clothes before eating, but still felt presentable with his fresh shave and combed hair. They enjoyed a hearty meal together, Hickey having a talent for reheating leftovers. Then they talked.

"What was Dominie VandeBruin's topic this morning?" Hickey asked.

"Domie Vannerbine preached off'n Lord's Day Three in the Hindyberg Cattychism," Albert responded, articulating carefully and to the best of his ability, obviously proud that he remembered such details. "He said God didn't make us evil, but we got that way when Adam and Eve got seduced by the serpent and ate the ferbitten fruit. He even talked about me. He said all our righteous is like the dirty rags I get from people and take to the Rag & Metal. We can't do nothin' good unless we got the Holy Spirit in us. And if we ain't got the Holy Spirit in us we can't do no good at all, but if we have, we won't do all the evil things the world does. Did I lissen good, Mr. Bishop?"

"You listened very well, Mr. Bosch. May I call you Albert? I'd like you to be my friend, and I'd like you to call me Edward. Can we do that?"

"I like that. I never had no friend before."

"Well, you have now. Albert, do you feel that you have the Spirit of the Lord living in you?" Albert didn't answer. "Do you believe you are an evil person, as the dominie said we all are?"

"I don't think much about it Mr., er, Edward. I just push my cart and buy junk from the people and bring it across the hill. I don't know if that is evil or not. I don't think so."

"No, your work is not evil, Albert, but what about your heart? What do you think about? Do you think lascivious or hateful thoughts?"

"I don't get sivious, I don't think, but I sometimes get het up when the boys pester me. They sometimes steal my stuff and make me buy it back from them. They think I don't know."

"That's understandable if you get upset. But do you hate them for it?"

"Oh no. They're just boys. They're just having fun. They don't mean nothing by it."

"What about the people you buy from. Do they treat you fairly?"

"I tell them what I give them for their old stuff. Sometimes they want more, but I say no. My price is firm. I don't hagger."

"And Mr. Amsterdam at the Rag & Metal. Does he treat you fairly?"

"Yes. He always asks me what I paid for my stuff, and he gives me more. He's a good man."

"Who are the good people in your life?"

"Oh, you are, Edward, and Miss Josie. The firemen are real good too. They fix my cart up and paint it and stuff. They bring me kerosene and see that my electric is on. Cap'n Pearce at Sodjers in the Cross, he's a real good man. And Mr. Benton, next door, he helps me a lot. He looks out for me. He's a good man too."

"I've got to meet him," Hickey said, with a positive nod of the head. Then he closed the conversation. "You are indeed a prince of a man, my friend. I've enjoyed our conversation, Albert, and I'm looking forward to more. Now I have to spend time reading and writing, if you'll excuse me."

Albert went home happy.

CHAPTER TWELVE

Anything for a Neighbor

The next morning after Albert left on his rounds, Hickey walked between the rows of Albert's collection of relics to visit Mr. Benton. He heard the scraping of a shovel coming from the barn so he stepped through the door.

Hickey had never been in a barn before, so the poignant smell of horses and manure was as new to him as the smell of whiskey on that fateful night at Gerdes's Tavern. At first it stung his eyes and forced him to hold his breath, but after a few minutes his system began to adjust and his mind began to accept the earthiness of his surroundings. He found Mr. Benton behind the horse stalls.

"Hello, Mr. Benton. My name is Edward Bishop. I've recently moved in two doors down, right beside Mr. Bosch."

"Yeah, I've heard of ya'," Mr. Benton answered. "Widda' Oosting's nephew. What can I do for ya'?"

"Since we're neighbors, I just thought to come over and make your acquaintance. Mr. Bosch is grateful for the help you give him. He speaks very highly of you."

"Oh, he does, 'eh?" said Mr. Benton, looking at Hickey quizzically.

"Yes, he puts you right in the same category as the firemen and Captain Pearce at the Soldiers of the Cross."

"Well, I guess I orta take that as a compliment," Mr. Benton replied, with a laugh as he threw another shovel full of manure through the window onto the pile outdoors.

"Why is it that I never smell the manure over at my place?" Hickey asked.

"I s'pose it's because you live upwind," he replied, again with a laugh. "The Dutch folks east of here ain't so lucky. They used to complain but it never did 'em no good. We're zoned for horses."

"These are work horses, are they not?"

"Oh yeah. They earn their oats all right. They are American saddle horses and old trotters. Cops use 'em on the beats downtown, and the dairy uses 'em to haul milk."

"Yes, I've seen them on the street."

"We use to have more. We used to keep 'em for the firehouse too, but they quit using horses altogether. I used to board ole Tipper's horse before he kicked the bucket. Ole sot never paid me," he laughed, "except for the old vegetables he gave me that he couldn't sell. He never made no money. I don't know how they made it. Every day he traded some vegetables for box meals for her and hisself at Soldiers of the Cross, and she used to do some washing and sewing, I think."

Hickey winced at the remembrance of their poverty, then changed the subject.

"Does Dominie VandeBruin ever pay you a visit?" Hickey asked.

"No. He came once, but I told him I wasn't Dutch, and he never came back."

"Are you a Christian? Do you go to church?" Hickey asked.

"Well, the Methodists married me and they'll probably bury me. Don't go to church 'cept for weddings and funerals. I look out for folks. Don't hurt nobody."

He ended the interrogation by walking over toward the grain bin and Hickey followed him, choosing not to pursue the matter of Mr. Benson's soul. There he noticed an old newspaper clipping tacked to the wall over the grain bin with a picture of young Benton in a baseball uniform and an old headline that read, *Benton Earns All-State honors in Base Ball*.

"So you're a ball player," Hickey said, studying the faded photo.

"Yeah, I played in school and played for a couple of years in the minors. Played in four different towns. Kept my satchel packed. Never made it to the bigs."

"I understand that Mr. Casien White, around the corner, also was a ball player. Did you and he ever play together?"

"Just when we was kids down at the lot. He was the best shortstop I ever seen. Could have played in the bigs if he was white. But he couldn't even play in the youth league when we was kids. Negroes can't get no sponsors."

"And they aren't allowed to play on teams with white boys?"

"Yeah. That's just how it is. It ain't wrote in the rules or nothing, but that's just how it is. It's a shame. Some of them boys is pretty good. And Ole Cass, he's a damn good teacher. Too bad he's a drunk."

Hickey winced. "Do the Negro boys have any hope?"

"If they're good enough, they might get into the Negro League like Cass did. You have to be pretty damn good to get in if you never played organized ball. They don't usually give no tryouts to boys who didn't play in kid leagues." Mr. Benton put away his shovel and leaned against a post as though prepared for a long conversation.

"How did Casien get in?"

"He was so good on the lots that everybody took notice, and the sports editor of the *Chronicle* wrote a letter to the Memphis Red Sox. That's how he got a tryout. He played for 'em just over a year, then he got beaned. That's what broke him."

"How does he get along?" Hickey asked, probing for information.

"They worked out some kind of settlement for him so he wouldn't sue. Them darkies fight amongst each other, but they look out for each other too, you know.

Kind of like the Dutch," he added with a mischievous grin. "You ain't Dutch, are you?"

Hickey avoided the question. "Do you and he see each other?" he asked.

"Oh, yeah. I go over to the yard and watch his boys practice. They learn a lot from Cass. He's a great teacher when he's sober. He won't take nobody unless a coach sends him. Every coach in town knows ole Cass." I'm superintendent of the Veterans' Association Youth League, you know. I keep all their records, schedule their games and hire the umps."

"I had no idea. That must be an important position."

"Yeah, I got a lot of responsibility. Good thing I got the time. They pay me a little to do all the legwork. It helps keep food on the table, if you know what I mean."

"If a Negro team had a sponsor, could they play in the league?"

"Sure they could, if they had a sponsor. But nobody around here is going to sponsor a Negro team. Their business would go to hell. This ain't the Harlem Globe Trotters, you know," he said with a laugh. "No Colored business in town big enough to sponsor a team," he added, "'cept the funeral director, and he won't touch it. Oh yeah, the Sepia, but the league wouldn't let them in."

"What does sponsorship cost?"

"By the time you buy every boy a shirt and hat, pay for bats, balls and catcher's equipment and pay the entry fee into the league to pay for umpires and other stuff, you may spend well over a hundred dollars. Maybe more if you buy good stuff."

"Does each team have its own field?"

"Some do. Usually they just play in schoolyards or in the city parks. We play our games on pretty good fields that have good backstops and benches. Sometimes after a hard rain we have puddles in the infield, but we get by."

"Who maintains the fields?"

"The Veterans' Association keeps 'em up. City likes that. We have a lot of volunteer help. Dads mow the outfields and rake the infields," he said, throwing a saddle on a brown mare. Just then a policeman wearing a blue uniform and black leather spats drove up. "That's Officer Dowd," Mr. Benton said. "He's come to get his horse."

Hickey found the arrival of Officer Dowd a good opportunity to take his leave. "Thank you for the conversation, Mr. Benton, I've enjoyed it. Learned a lot, too. Thank you for the education."

"Anything for a neighbor," Mr. Benton laughed.

And Hickey walked thoughtfully back home, happy that he had made Mr. Benton's acquaintance. "A good man," he said to himself, "a Christian heart without the knowledge."

CHAPTER THIRTEEN

wiskie for edwerd

Albert, Josie, Mr. Benton and we boys were the only people who had access to Hickey's back door, and his back yard was not accessible from the street. The postman and the paperboy were the only people who ever approached his front door, and both used the mail slot for their pickups and deliveries. Hickey read the *Chronicle* from cover to cover every day and soon was as conversant with life in the town as anyone. The mailman delivered his denominational journals, his magazines, his bills, his monthly bank statements and other business mail, and picked up his outgoing letters. The iceman and the kerosene man both made their deliveries next door at Albert's, and the electric meter was at the front of the house. He took ice from Albert's box, got his kerosene from Albert's tank and put it in his cook stove and heater with a funnel. He had successfully arranged the details of a reclusive life for himself, severely limiting access by the outside world and keeping only fundamental company. And he was content. Well, reasonably content until something triggered the craving that began to gnaw at his mind, his belly, his bones, and his very soul.

Late one afternoon when Albert had finished his rounds, Hickey knocked on his door with the cardboard back of a writing pad in his hand. "Albert, my friend, I have a very special favor to ask of you." Albert looked up and smiled a consenting smile. "Remember when I told you that from time to time I may have need for some whiskey? Well, I'd like you to write on this cardboard these words: 'Whiskey for Edward.' I'd like you to keep this card wedged behind one of the boards in your shed, printed side hidden, of course. If, on a given morning you find the sign lying on your cart, printed side up, you are to put the sign back behind the board and on your rounds stop at Petrone's and give the storekeeper the envelope you'll find under the sign. It will contain a note and a check. He will give you the whiskey in a paper bag and an envelope with some change in it. Will you do that for me, my friend, and bring me the whiskey and the cash?"

"Are you going to make some boyungus?" Albert asked, grinning.

"No, Albert, no Boeren Jongens."

"Elder Fles tole me once that whiskey was okay for medicine and boyungus, but not for drinkin'."

"Yes, my friend, the old Dutch have ways of justifying the things they do. It's okay to eat raisins stewed in whiskey, but it is improper to drink it from a glass. They have their ways."

He gave Albert the cardboard from a pad of writing paper, and satisfied that by letters to the storekeeper at Petrone's, he had successfully arranged the procurement of his alcohol, he said good night and went home.

Albert dutifully laid the cardboard on his dining table, got out an oversized pencil such as kindergarteners use, and wrote, in a childish scrawl, *wiskie for edwerd,* retracing each of the letters several times.

CHAPTER FOURTEEN

The Only Flaw in Paradise

One Tuesday afternoon about a month after Josie began working for him, she appeared at his back door with swollen, watery eyes. "What's wrong, Josie, are you afflicted with spring allergies or is something grieving you?"

"It's me and Casien," she answered. "He know his settlement done run out and he know I go away ever day after he go down town. Now he think I be 'ho'in'. I tell him I be working honest, cookin' and cleanin'. He ask me where, and I say the rich white folk I work for don't want nobody to know. He think I be lyin'."

"Oh, my dear Josie," he said, with frustration, sitting down on the couch, "we have a dilemma." Neither spoke for a time, each looking off in opposite directions. He broke the silence. "We must resolve this problem. You cannot live in distrust with your husband, but neither can I have it known publicly that you frequent my home. The world would not understand. Can we trust your husband to keep our confidence?"

"Casien not my husban'," she offered. "We never get married in a church or nothin'. We was going to but then he got hurt and we never did. So we just take care of one another," she declared with her usual candidness and sat on the couch beside him.

He paused, unsure how to pursue the matter. He decided on boldness. "You do share a bed, do you not?"

"Well, Casien go to sleep right after supper, and when it dark I have to push him over to get in the bed. In the mornin' all he want to do is get up and go out. He have his breakfas' and leave for the play yard."

"Are you telling me you and Casien are not one flesh?" he asked.

"Me and Casien do it all the time when we was in Memphis, but he don't get up to it no more. Ever since he got hurt in the head and took to drinkin'. I don't think he a man no more, but he good. He love his boys and he never hurt me. We never talk about nothin' no more. He just drink. But he do kiss me goodbye ever day."

"So you are not another man's wife," he whispered as an aside to himself, then he put his arm around her to console her and she leaned against him. She was soft and warm, comforting and inviting, and she stirred him with her candid talk.

"Here we sit, Mr. Edward. You and me, and ain't neither of us really got nobody else, really. We is and we isn't. We both be alone. Bein' alone ain't no good."

"It is not good for man to be alone," he quoted as he drew her closer and she laid her face on his chest, "the only flaw in paradise. God provided a remedy then... and now...."

Forces beyond their control took over, and she made love to him there on the couch. Both were empty and craved affection, he without really knowing it. He was inept, and she gifted in the art of lovemaking, and they both knew it instinctively, so he submitted as she guided him down the path to his first encounter, which was clumsy to say the least.

Passions tore at him, torrents of guilt and ecstasy clashed over him. An old song about angry surges rolling on his tempest driven soul echoed in his head. *I'm perishing*, he thought, *my anchor can no longer hold*. The flood devoured him. He lost his breath. Then the calm.

When it was over she lay beside him smiling.

"Mr. Edward, I think you be a virgin," she said with a mischievous grin.

"Yes, Josie," he answered, grateful for the comic relief, "this was the maiden voyage of the *HMS Bisschop*. I'm afraid she floundered a bit in the billows, and the captain embarrassed himself. A *Bisschop* who couldn't sail the *Zee*. What a telling metaphor."

"That's okay, Mr. Edward," she responded, still grinning, "you gets better with 'sperience. All the mens do."

He took that to be her statement of intent to continue their relationship. She rose, cleaned herself and went on with her chores, softly singing a tune he didn't recognize, one he thought beautiful but discordant with the music echoing in his head. She stopped singing and smiled at him.

"My mind is in a tempest, dear Josie," he said. "I need rest."

"I think you be a tempes' in a teapot, Mr. Edward, yo' face be hard but yo' heart be sof'."

He lay on the couch trying to sleep, trying to dream, trying to fantasize about life as a professor, trying to imagine Josie as an esteemed professor's respected wife, trying anything to escape the contradictions of the moment. He decided to go for a walk.

He walked the entire length of the two-track eastward to Getty, gazing down on the celery flats watching the farmers weeding the celery below. He found a shady spot on the hillside and sat for a long time pondering alternatives. The more he thought, the more addled his brain became. The straight, orderly rows of new celery screamed mockeries at him.

He had never faced a moral dilemma. Never before had two such opposing forces torn him apart. In the academic world all was theoretical. Choices were always easy. Moses, St. Paul and John Calvin had seen to that. Even when he fled from the seminary, the choice was easy. There was no alternative. But now his heart and his conscience were at war, and his body sided with his heart. *I'm perishing*, he thought, then he said it aloud, "I'm perishing."

Of one thing he was sure. He couldn't let Josie go. It was too late for that. But yet the struggle continued.

What could he do? Could he send Josie packing? No, what if she never returned? That thought terrified him. Under what circumstances could she come and live with him? Could he kill Casien? Unthinkable. He might be caught and go to jail. Then what would Josie do? And you can't drink in jail. Could he kill himself? Unthinkable too. People who murder or commit suicide may not go to heaven. But what if they are insane? And what about King David? Oh yes, the punishment. His thoughts soared far beyond the realm of reason. After a long while and without solution, he rose and went home, expecting her to be gone. But she wasn't.

When he entered his back door he found her sitting on the couch, crying. "I think you be leaving me." she said. "Do you want I don't come back?"

"No, dear Josie, no. I want you to stay. I mean, I want you to come back, tomorrow and every day."

"What I tell Casien?" she asked.

"Do you have to tell him anything? Can't we go on as we are?"

"Like nothin' happen?"

"Yes... well, no, dear Josie. You stay where you are and take care of Casien and continue to come here every day as you do until we can make sense of this thing."

"This ain't like 'ho'in'," she declared. "'Ho'in' don't mean nothin'. It just for the money. This ain't like 'ho'in', Mr. Edward. This ain't like 'ho'in'. I don't know what I do. I can't leave Casien, I don't know what he do. I owe him. He a good man. And you a good man, Mr. Edward...." And she began to cry again and he sat beside her on the couch and put his arm around her. "You take care of me, Mr. Edward. I take care of you, and you take care of me. And we both take care of Casien and Mr. Albert."

Neither said a word for a long minute. Then she spoke again. "Do I be a 'ho now?"

"No, my dear Josie. You're not a...," he couldn't say the word outside its scriptural context, "...you are a woman of virtue and you should be clothed in scarlet."

She stiffened. "But 'ho's wears red," she retorted.

"Scarlet is the symbol of honor and nobility. Prostitutes wear red to feign nobility, or to mock it, I don't know which."

Understanding passed her by. "We need one another. You and me and Casien and Mr. Albert. We need one another."

"I know, dear Josie, I know. We all need each other, and we all take care of each other. That is our calling. We are like a couple and Albert and Casien are our children. It's getting late. You had better go home. We'll think on this again tomorrow."

"This all make me crazy, Mr. Edward, this all just make me crazy."

"It worries me too, Josie, it does. But we must maintain our sanity. There has to be a proper solution to our quandary. Let me ponder it during the night.

And Josie, please just call me Edward. Drop the mister. I deserve no title."

She slowly packed her picnic basket and left.

Albert came home late in the afternoon as usual, but tonight they ate in silence, Hickey being unwilling to initiate conversation. Then they parted company. Hickey tossed and turned all night.

The next morning, Albert opened his shed and saw on the bed of his cart the piece of cardboard turned up. He shuddered, but set out to do his friend's bidding.

CHAPTER FIFTEEN

The Only Tenderness

That afternoon Josie appeared later than usual, this time dressed in slacks and flowered top rather than her usual black dress. "Had trouble yesterday, Mr. Edward," she began immediately upon arriving. "Casien go the wrong way on Wood Street and get lost and go all the way to 'Brosia. The polices bring him home. I can't trus' him no more. Some day he get los' and I never see him again. What I do, Mr. Edward?"

"Well," he paused and thought for a moment, "how much does a taxi cost?"

"From the Sepia home Avery charge thirty cent. Avery the Color taxi man. He reasonable, but we ain't got that much for every day."

"If it would give you peace of mind, dear Josie, I would be happy to pay for his cab ride home. You could give the saloonkeeper the money and he could arrange it. He is a respectable fellow, is he not? Maybe we could also increase Casien's daily allowance so he could stay a little longer."

"Yes, Mr. Gile' at the Sepia, he be okay. He take care of Casien. Casien be his reglarist customer, I think. If you give him more money, he just get drunker. But if you say so, Mr. Edward."

"Please remember, Josie, just call me Edward."

"Yes, sir," she answered, unwilling, it seemed, to deprive him entirely of title.

Josie left Hickey's house early that day to make the arrangement. That afternoon, just about the time Cass's dollar ran out, Josie brought a cash advance to Mr. Giles, and he agreed to call the taxi for him late each afternoon. Cass was too drunk to comprehend what was going on. She sat on the barstool next to him and nursed a glass of ginger ale while he finished his last beer. Then she rode home with him in Avery's taxi much as a mother would ride home with her child on the bus after the first day of kindergarten.

That same afternoon Albert returned with two fifths of whiskey. He and Hickey ate supper in silence. Hickey excused Albert early on the pretense that he had some reading and writing to do. When Albert left, Hickey opened one of his bottles and began to drink slowly, savoring each drop. As the haze began to grow around his head, he began to drink more greedily, losing track of time and his surroundings.

He sipped and dozed lightly all through the night. Each time he fell asleep, bizarre dreams tormented him. Seminarians mocked him, Japanese Zeroes bombed his house, German soldiers kicked down his door and invaded his privacy, tramps who came in from the two-track stole his food, and the pope forgave his sins of gluttony and drunkenness. As day dawned he arose in a stupor and staggered through his back yard and Albert's, preaching like he'd never preached before, loudly condemning all the evils that engulfed him.

That same day as Cass was leaving for the Sepia, Josie pressed not only a dollar but another twenty five cents into his hand, telling him that she had done good work on her job and that the rich white people had given her a raise and that he would be able to stay a little longer and have two more glasses of beer before his cab ride home. He bristled at the mention of rich white people, but since his needs were being met and he could get more beer, did not protest. "Just be sure you ain't 'ho'in'," Josie reported him to have said. "Just be sure you ain't 'ho'in'. If you be 'ho'in' I be killin' somebody." And she assured him that she wasn't.

When she neared Hickey's house that afternoon, she could hear him clear down to the two-track. He was raging drunk. As she paused on the path, uncertain what to do, Calvin and I rode up on our bikes. Excited by the commotion, we scrambled up the bank toward his house and saw him in his back yard ranting and raving. It was the first time we had seen him drunk.

He raged against Satan. He raged against poverty. He raged against the evils of Catholicism. He raged against the Jews for denying their Messiah and for causing the depression. He raged against his ancestors for bringing Negro slaves to America. He raged against the church for its greed and for various heresies, ranting that the Whore of Babylon had taken over the church. He raged against creeping socialism in the government and he raged against Germany, Japan and Italy. His rage was all mixed together incoherently, and as he ranted he stumbled around, kicking at clods of earth and reeling and nearly falling down. He wandered into Albert's yard and kicked at the stoves and the iceboxes as though they were squads of enemy soldiers, then he staggered back into his own yard, laboriously climbed his three back steps while clinging to the post, and sat down in the overstuffed chair on his back porch. Then he was quiet. Queen Anne told us boys to run off, and she climbed the embankment to go to his aid.

She stooped beside him and kissed his forehead. "Lovie gon' take care of you," she whispered, "Lovie gon' take good care of you."

Somehow she knew better than to antagonize him or to get him to stop drinking. She knew it had to run its course, so she nursed him through the binge and nursed him through the withdrawal.

She was the only tenderness he knew.

CHAPTER SIXTEEN

Sunday at Calvin's

Every other Sunday, Calvin and I would go to each other's house for dinner. The Sunday dinner menu was the same in both houses, and I surmise that it was the same in all Dutch homes. Beef roast, potatoes and gravy, green beans, carrots or corn, with pudding or sometimes pie for dessert. With the exception of the variation in vegetables, it was always the same. The roast at Calvin's house was always cooked just right, and I liked it better than the roast my mother cooked. The roast at my house was always overcooked, crisp and dry. You had to soak it in gravy to get it juicy. Calvin liked the roast at my house a lot better than his mother's. I don't know why, except that he said it was nice and crunchy.

The menu was the only thing common to both our homes. There the similarity stopped. At my house we ate in the kitchen, on wooden chairs around the old wooden table we had inherited from my mother's parents. The table was protected by an old, cracked oilcloth and the hot dishes were placed on hand woven hot pads to keep them from sticking to the oilcloth. Our silverware was mismatched, mother's fork being small and dainty, dad's being heavy, and the rest a mixture. But we each had our own. Mother served the roast and the potatoes on dinner plates and the gravy and vegetables in cereal bowls. She stacked the bread on a saucer and put the butter on the table in its wrapper. My dad always took his Sunday shirt off to avoid soiling it, and ate dinner in his undershirt.

At Calvin's house we ate in the dining room, on padded chairs around a large oval oak table, covered with a white linen tablecloth and centered directly under a crystal chandelier. We ate off real china, and every piece matched. The serving dishes had little feet on them, eliminating the need for hot pads. The silverware was real engraved silver, and every piece matched. The roast was served on a large platter, the vegetables and potatoes in covered bowls, and the gravy in a gravy boat whose cover had a notch for the ladle. Rolls were served in a basket covered with a linen napkin and the butter in a large rectangular server. The dominie always wore his formal, black, double breasted preaching suit to dinner and tucked a napkin in at his neck.

Calvin would rather be at my house than at his own, even though his was much nicer. My house was plain and square. The only beauty was the flowerbeds that my parents lovingly cultivated all summer long. Inside, the rooms were neat and nicely decorated with wallpaper and pictures and plaques. The floors were covered with linoleum. We had plain pine woodwork. Our windows had pull down shades, except for the living room. It had Venetian blinds. The furniture was old, and had a used look, the sofa and dad's chair being lumpy and the cushions uneven. Our screened-in porch was in front of the house, and we had a swing whose chains squeaked. My parents liked to sit there on summer evenings and chat with people who walked by.

Calvin's house was a classic old manse that stood next to the church. It was, by far, the finest house on Ambrosia Avenue. The rooms were twice the size of ours, with textured plaster walls, soft carpets, bay windows and lace and velvet draperies. Flower shapes were carved into the dark oak woodwork. The furniture looked as though it were still new, fresh from the store. The pillars out front matched the huge pillars of the church and framed the big bay windows of the living and dining rooms. Their screened-in porch was behind the house, off the kitchen, where they could sit out of the public eye. And they had a garage for their big black Buick that I never got to ride in.

Calvin's house had flowerbeds too, but his parents never tended them. Retired people from the church's building and grounds committee mowed the lawns and tended the gardens. I never saw the dominie dressed in anything but a suit and tie. And whereas the other Dutch ladies wore housedresses during the week and Sunday dresses on Sunday, Calvin's mother wore Sunday dresses all week long.

Every Monday the dominie got up early and took the big black Buick for a two hour drive to the seminary where he conducted a seminar for students and sat on the ministerial approval board. Beyond that, his reputation for righteous living and powerful preaching earned him a seat on the seminary's Board of Governors. In his capacity as a governor, he persuaded the board to honor his hero Pieter Bisschop by naming the new seminary library in his honor, since he was renown as an author and had, since his departure, contributed so generously to the seminary, though no one had since had contact with him, unaware of his circumstance back in the Old Country since the Nazi occupation.

And Calvin's mother spent every Monday at the home of Mrs. Dr. Voordthuisen, who lived in a big, fancy house across the street from the hospital. Dr. and Mrs. Voordthuisen were pillars of our church, and Mrs. Voordthuisen was president of the Ladies' Guild. Together they drank tea and planned the events for the ladies of the church. Every week while Mrs. VandeBruin was away, ladies from the congregation came and cleaned her house.

Other than being Dutch and belonging to the same church, our parents were nothing alike. My dad was a sports fan. We played basketball behind the garage, played catch in the back yard and listened to the Tiger games on the radio. Often my dad and I wrestled. We had a wonderful physical relationship. Mother was the spiritual leader in our home. She made sure we knew our catechism and prepared our memory work for Sunday school.

In Calvin's home, his father was the boss. He never called him dad, always father or sir, and I always called him dominie. He always called me Christian, and called his own children by their given names, Calvin and Grace. He called his wife Mrs. VandeBruin. He never played basketball or catch, and I never saw him without a suit and tie. He and Calvin never wrestled.

Calvin had one thing I envied, a Lionel train set with a crossing gate that went up and down and a car that could dump its load of coal when you pressed the button. My parents couldn't afford a train set, but if they could have, my dad would have played with me. Unless he had a friend over, Calvin had to play alone.

One thing was the same in both homes: Sunday noon dinner was always accompanied by discussion. The children were expected to summarize the sermon, to report on their Sunday school lesson, and to recite their memory work. After we had cleaned our plates, the inquisition would begin, and, being good children, we were always prepared. Even Gracie answered questions about the sermon and recited her texts for the dominie.

I ate at Calvin's house the Sunday after Hickey's drunk. That day Gracie reported that her Sunday school lesson was about the poor widow who faithfully cast her last farthing into the treasury, even though she had no money left for food. Dominie VandeBruin used that opportunity to praised the memory of old Widow Oosting, whom he claimed faithfully placed a nickel in the offering plate, when he knew for a certainty that it was the only coin she had in her purse. He reminded all of us that tithing was one of the most significant signs of Christian sincerity. We could sing in church, learn our lessons and keep the Sabbath perfectly, but opening our purse to the Lord was discipleship of the highest order.

Then it was Mrs. VandeBruin's turn to report on the events of her week. Being the spiritual director of the Ladies' Guild, she reported the essence of the meeting, the lesson topic, who prepared coffee and cake, and what of importance the ladies discussed.

That Sunday, the discussion was lively. "Mrs. Baker shocked us all by describing what went on at Drunkard Bishop's house last week," she reported, casually using the word drunkard as a title.

"Did he make a nuisance of himself?" the dominie asked.

"She said that he cursed and swore and went on a violent verbal rampage condemning everything from the government to the church, including Negroes, Jews, communists, and even the poor iceman."

"How long did it continue," he asked.

"She said that it went on day and night for the rest of the week, and that he didn't stop until sunrise today."

"How does he know anything of the church?" he wondered aloud. "He can't possibly have ever set foot in one."

"Maybe he has a radio, and listens to the church broadcasts," she suggested.

"Or maybe it's the devil talking through him. I think that's it," he declared with authority. "They should have called the police and had him put in jail. There must be laws against that sort of thing. Did any children hear him?"

Calvin and I cast a knowing glance at each other, thrilled to have shared a moment beyond what our parents knew we had experienced, and thrilled to have tasted what they would forbid us to taste.

"I doubt it. Mrs. Baker said she went to the front sidewalk to see if he could be heard on the street, and she said you could hear him faintly but couldn't make out his words."

The dominie looked at us and repeated what he had said before. "You boys don't go anywhere near that place. The man is possessed by the devil himself. If you have to go down Amity Street, pass by on the other side of his house. And hurry. Those demons have a way of getting loose and getting into other people."

After the discussion, the dominie read the meditation for the day from Professor Pieter Bisschop's daily devotional. The thought for the day, taken from the Apostles' Creed, was that one day Jesus will return to earth to judge the living and the dead. Our job, according to the meditation, is to love and serve even "the least of these" without prejudice.

"That is easy for Professor Bisschop to say," the dominie mused. "As much as I admire that man, I'm sure he never had to live in the same neighborhood as a demon possessed drunkard, and just a few blocks from the depraved Negroes."

Changing the subject, Mrs. VandeBruin asked her husband, "Are you ready for your Sabbath rest dear?"

"More than ready," he responded, slightly relaxing his stern countenance, pushing his chair back and rising from the table. He carefully removed his suit coat and hung it neatly over the back of his chair. Then he untied his black bow tie, draped it neatly over the shoulder of his coat, and loosened the top button of his starched white shirt. Then he followed her up the wide, open stairway to the bedroom. It was about the only time I had ever seen him smile.

Mrs. VandeBruin stopped half way up, and he passed her on the stairway, moving faster than his usual measured gait. "Grace, dear, you go to your room, close the door and read the book I've put on your bed," she directed, "I'll quiz you on it at four o'clock. Boys, you stay in Calvin's room and study your catechism together, quietly. I'll quiz you when I've finished with Grace." She followed him up the stairs, removing the combs from her hair.

CHAPTER SEVENTEEN

A Glass of Tea

That Sunday Hickey awoke feeling exactly the way he felt after his first binge back at the seminary. He lay on his bed fully clothed, shirt and trousers twisted and hair matted. He couldn't stand the smell of himself. He was sick and his hands shook. He was hungry, but afraid to eat for fear he might begin to vomit and go into convulsions. Besides, there was only cold beef roast in the icebox, and the mere thought of it made him nauseous. Water tasted terrible, but the whiskey was gone and it being Sunday, no liquor stores were open. That was okay, because he knew he had to stop drinking or he might die. Even though he had lost track of time, he knew by instinct that it was Sunday, and didn't want to drink on Sunday anyway. Lacking the strength even to go outdoors, he slumped onto the couch and stayed there most of the day, napping from time to time. He didn't even notice when Albert came in to check on him late in the afternoon.

Albert had dressed himself that morning and had gone to church, but since he had no expectation of discussing the sermon with Hickey barely paid attention to the prayer, the scripture or the message. He was distraught. Hickey's binge had unsettled him. No, terrified him. His newfound sense of security had been ripped from him, and he felt responsible because he had provided the whiskey.

After church he walked downtown to the Soldiers of the Cross for lunch and not wanting to go home, in his confusion and loneliness, decided to turn off at Wood Street to visit Josie.

He knocked on her front door. There was no answer. He waited and knocked again. Again no answer. Assuming no one was home, he walked around the side toward the two-track, figuring he might as well take the back way home. He was surprised to hear her call to him from her back porch.

"Mr. Albert, why what are you doing in these parts on Sunday? I don't hardly recognize you on the street without your wagon."

"I thought I'd come by and see you, Miss Josie," Albert shouted from the two-track, "and I don't do no business on Sunday."

"Well, come on up. My, don't you look fine in that fancy suit! You buy that at The Toggery?" she said with a teasing laugh.

"No, you made it for me. Don't you 'member?"

"'Course, I 'member. I jus' be joshing you. I make a pitcher of ice tea. Would you like some?"

"I don't know. I never drunk no ice tea before," he said, walking toward her porch.

"We put some sugar in it. I think you like it."

She offered him a seat and a glass of tea. He took a sip and nodded in the affirmative. "It's good. Thank you. What gonna come of Mr. Edward?" he asked. "Ain't he gonna ever be sober no more?"

"He drink different than Casien," she offered. "I think he go on a toot ever now and 'gain when he get riled 'bout somethin'. I think he be okay when his whiskey run out and he get over the shakes."

"Will he be the same? Will he have me over to eat and talk?"

"Oh, I sure he will," she assured him. "Just give him a day or so to get his head put back on. He be okay."

"But I brung him the whiskey, Miss Josie. I brung it to him. It's my fault."

"No, Mr. Albert, It ain't your fault. It ain't nobody fault. It just how it is. Sometimes a man have to drink to forget his miseries. It just how it is. If you don't get him the whiskey, he might die of the cravin'. You a good man, Mr. Albert. You a good friend to Mr. Edward. You take care of him and he take care of you. We all take care one of another. Mr. Edward need his groceries and his whiskey. You take care of him. You need your supper. We take care of you. Mr. Edward say we be call to do it. He be okay."

Albert felt relieved. Very much relieved.

Cass appeared in the doorway, rubbing his good eye. Josie stood up. His sudden appearance flustered her. "I thought you be sleepin'," she said sharply.

"You talkin' wake me up," he answered. "What you be doin' on my back stoop, Mr. Junkman?" he asked. Albert couldn't respond. "An' you be wearin' my suit. Why you be wearin' my suit?"

"We sole Mr. Bosch that suit a long time ago," she lied. "You just don't 'member 'cuz you brain be stewed with beer."

"Why we sole him my good meetin' suit?" he asked.

"'Cuz you don't go to church no more, and Mr. Bosch he need a church suit. So we sole it to him. Besides, you need the money for your drinkin'."

"So, why you be sittin' on my stoop drinkin' my tea and yakking wif' my woman, Mr. Junkman?" he asked, sullenly.

"He just stop by to see what he should do about the man who live next door to him. He be drinkin'," she intervened, taking Albert off the hook. "He know that I know how to take care of a drinkin' man." Then turning to Albert, "Don't mine him, he just talk bad 'cause it Sunday and he can't go to the Sepia. You take some of Josie's ice tea to yo' neighbor man. It make him feel better."

She went inside and got a full jug of tea from the ice box. "Give him a glass of this," she said, "it make him feel better."

Albert was only too happy to leave. He took the jug of tea and headed down the two-track toward home. He went straight to Hickey's house and went inside. Hickey was draped on the couch, snoring. Albert poured a glass of tea from the jug and left it on the table. He put the jug in the icebox and went home.

CHAPTER EIGHTEEN

A Family Thing

Late Monday morning Hickey woke up on his couch, still hung over but feeling a bit better than Sunday. He looked over toward the table and saw the glass of iced tea that Albert had brought the day before. He took a sip, thinking it might be whiskey, then sniffed it, and discovered it was tea. It was warm, but refreshing, so he added a few ice chips and drank it down slowly.

He was hungry, but dared not put food into his queasy stomach. With a pencil in his hand, he spent the morning making notes on his ubiquitous yellow pad, recording his feelings and the memory of his stupor. He didn't move from his chair until Josie climbed his steps that afternoon.

Without a word she went to the icebox and poured him a fresh glass of cold tea, and while he sipped quietly she warmed some leftover beef and made him a sandwich. They ate in silence, he pondering his drunkenness and she in deep thought about the complications of her life. She spoke first.

"Casien 'spec somethin'," Josie said as she put their dishes in the sink. "Mr. Albert come over yesterday and Casien hear us talkin' about you gettin' drunk. Then he see Mr. Albert wearin' his ole suit and he see me give him some ice tea for you. Then he talk about gettin' more drinkin' money and the taxi and all. He 'spec somethin'."

"What did you tell him?" he asked.

"I tell him he ain't got no mine lef' in his head, that he drink it all away."

"Oh, don't be abrasive to him, Josie, just humor him. As long as he gets his fill of beer he will be content, I believe. If he no longer desires you for conjugal purposes, he shouldn't be too concerned about your comings and goings. Just be kind to him, assure him of your constancy, and send him on his way every day, just as before. He'll soon forget about the suit and the iced tea and Mr. Bosch's visit. He'll soon forget."

"I hope so," she said. "But I won't forget. I be a livin' lie. I be lettin' him think he be my man when he ain't my man no more. You be my man now, Edward. You be my man, and I glad you be my man. But I live with Casien and I sleep with Casien, even if he don't get up to it no more. He still think I be his woman. That make me crazy, Edward, that make me crazy." And she began to cry.

He took her in his arms. "I'm happy that you are my woman, Josie. And I'm honored to be your man. And I don't want you to be crazy. Things will work out for us, I'm sure they will, somehow." He wanted to add, "with God's help," but thought the better of it.

They made love again, this time on the bed and this time better than before. Still weak and a bit shaky from the binge, he was not so hasty. He was more relaxed and she less assertive, allowing him to take the lead. It was good, and it lasted.

This time, when it was finished, he didn't go for a walk. He stayed in the house and they sat and lingered over the iced tea that Albert had brought over on Sunday.

"I put tea bags on the lis' nex time Mr. Albert go shoppin'," she said.

"That would be good. I like tea."

"I know why Casien drink, but I don't know why you drink, Edward," she said, dropping the mister for the first time. "Why you drink?"

"Why does Casien drink?" he asked, reverting to the tactics of the debater.

"He drink because his heart be broke," she answered. "Most of anythin' he want to play ball and he be good, but he get his head busted and can't play ball no more. It break his heart so he drink. He have to. Do your heart be broke, Edward?"

"No, my heart isn't broke, dear Josie, my heart isn't broke. I'm resigned to my destiny. I'm not sure what it is with me. Maybe it's a family thing. My mother died bearing me and my father died soon after from drinking. My only living relative was my Aunt Ella Oosting, who lived right here in this very house. Her husband drank too. The people around here called him Tipper."

"The folk here call you Hickey," she interjected.

He frowned, "She was my mother's sister," he continued, "but she couldn't afford to take me in. The Dutch orphanage took me in and she would come to visit me about once a month. I visited her sometimes in the summer, right here in this very house. I always liked it here. I remember Mr. Bosch from when I was a youngster. And he remembers me, but didn't remember it was I who used to visit here. Anyway, she told me that my grandfather, whom I never knew, also drank. So, I think the thorn in my flesh is a family infirmity.

"The orphanage raised me and educated me. They sent me to Canada to boarding school when I was fourteen and I earned a scholarship to college and to the seminary. Then I earned a doctorate while serving as a graduate assistant at the seminary."

"You be a doctor?" she asked excitedly.

"No, not a medical doctor," he answered. "I am a doctor of theology." He paused and smiled broadly, "I studied God. Then I became a professor at the seminary. Look what my Aunt Ella gave me," he said, going to one of his beer cartons and exhuming the brass nameplate. "This must have cost her a small fortune, and she could ill afford it."

She looked at him, admiringly, but without understanding. "You be a mystery, Edward. How you study God? He let you in his big house in the sky to look at him and ax him questions?"

"No, Josie, just in books and papers. It's more philosophy than science. I was a professor of theology in the seminary, but I took to drink and had to sever my relationship with the institution. Yes, in retrospect, I think my heart was somewhat broken by that severance, but with your gentle care, it is beginning to mend."

She gave up trying to understand. "But why you drink if your heart ain't broke bad and be mendin'?"

"I can't explain it Josie. I never drank until that one night at the seminary. It started quite by accident. It was the finest feeling I ever had, that is until you came into my life. You make me feel better than the whiskey does."

"Well, I'm glad of that. Maybe now you don't drink no more?"

"I don't want to drink, Josie, but sometimes the compulsion gets so strong that I can't resist. Do you understand that?"

"Like a hog in heat?"

"Yes, I suppose, like a hog in heat," he laughed.

"Casien don't be like a hog in heat. He just be like a hog. He wake up ever mornin' and just go to the play yard. Then when the whistle blow he go downtown and drink. He can't do nothin' else. They's his two loves, ball and beer. But you don't be like Casien, Edward, you be smart and you talk good and you read and you write on that tablet. Casien, he just grunt 'cep when he be talkin' to his boys in the school yard. Then he talk good."

"Well, I hope I never take to grunting, Josie, but if you keep cooking as you do, I may begin to look like a hog. I'm sleepy my dear, I think I'd like a nap."

"You go on ahead and snooze, Edward, while I fix up this mess of a place. You get to drinkin' and your house look like Mr. Bosch's junkyard."

He returned to the couch and, while she restored order to the room, slept for two hours before she woke him up.

"I'm hungry, my dear, what do we have to eat?"

"We still got some chops in the icebox. Would you like some chops?"

"That sounds wonderful. Pork for the pig. Oink." He laughed, and so did she.

While she cooked, he resumed writing and soon filled a pad with the myriad of thoughts that consumed him. He wrote about his youth, his education and his drinking. He wrote about coming to Hackley and wrote in detail of his experiences with Albert and with Josie. He wrote until Albert came home for supper. Without his writing, I would never have been able to write this story.

CHAPTER NINETEEN

Soldiers of the Cross

On Tuesday morning as Albert wheeled his cart out of the shed and around the back corner of his house, he noticed a man dressed in khaki slipping a note into the crack beside the screen.

"Cap'n Pearce!" he shouted.

"Hello, Albert. I thought I'd missed you. Saw you at lunch Sunday for the first time in quite a while, so I thought I'd stop by to see how you are."

"Oh, I'm fine, Cap'n Pearce. Just fine. 'Cept my neighbor, Edward, took to drinking last week so I couldn't eat by him. He's okay now though."

"Does he give you trouble?"

"Oh no. He's a good man, 'cept when he drinks. When he's sober he's a fine man. He has me over for dinner on Sundays and for supper the other days. Miss Josie, Cass White's wife, she cooks for us, and she made my church suit. Edward and me, we always talk after church about Domie Vannerbine's sermon and stuff. He's my friend. When he drinks, he gets nasty, but he don't hurt nobody. Just cusses and kicks stuff."

"What's his name?"

"Edward. Edward Bishop."

"Let's pay him a visit."

Together they walked across the back yard and knocked on Hickey's door.

"Is that you Albert?" Hickey asked from inside.

"Yes Edward, its me and Cap'n Pearce. Cap'n Pearce, from the Sodjers of the Cross."

Hickey wished that Captain Pearce had come another time. He had just got out of bed, was untidy, and had not shaved since the week before. Nevertheless he came to the door and opened it.

"Captain Pearce, It's my pleasure to meet you," Hickey said, extending a hand of welcome. "Please pardon my, ah, appearance. I've been a little ill of late," he said, sliding one of the heavy wooden chairs from the table. "Please sit."

"Are you alright now, Mr. Bishop?" Pearce asked, pulling out a chair and sitting down. "Is there anything I can do for you? Are you in need of anything?"

"No, sir, I'll be fine, thank you. I think I'd like a glass of iced tea, gentlemen, would you be so kind as to join me? Sit down, Albert, I'll get it."

Albert pulled out a chair and sat as Hickey walked gingerly to the icebox to get the jug of tea. He removed two more glasses from the cupboard and, after chipping some ice from the block, poured each of the others a glass.

"Tell me about the Soldiers of the Cross, Captain Pearce."

"We are a Christian charitable organization. We try to meet the basic needs of those society has discarded. And we look after the indigent, the widows and the fatherless. We provide meals for shut ins and serve about thirty souls each day in our dining room. We do what we can to fulfill Christ's mandate to feed the hungry, clothe the naked and tend the sick. We used to provide meals for the Oostings who lived here, and to the Widow Oosting after her husband died. Albert used to eat with us at noon, but I understand he eats with you now."

"Yes, he does. We enjoy each other's company. Albert is a fine man." At that remark, Albert beamed.

"Mr. Bishop, I understand that you drink?" Captain Pearce said with the inflection of a question.

"Yes, sir, from time to time I do. I can't explain it. A compulsive need sometimes comes over me and possesses me, a need that will not be satisfied until I take a drink or two. I think it is a family infirmity."

"That could well be, Mr. Bishop." he said with a positive nod. "When the compulsion attacks, perhaps you could contact me and I could come over and help you get through it. I'm told that it will pass."

But at that point Hickey was unwilling to seek a cure for his "thorn in the flesh," as he called it. To him the only way to relieve the temptation was to yield to it. He doubted if he could find the company of

Captain Pearce as fulfilling as a glass of whiskey when the need came. So he changed the subject.

"Captain, tell me more about the Soldiers of the Cross. Do you have a staff and a building?"

"We used to have a full time staff of four people, but then the depression hit and now the war. As the need for our services increased, our ability to deliver decreased. I thank God that the government set up soup kitchens, or many of our citizens would have starved, I think."

"Did the churches help at all?"

"Oh, the Catholics and the Methodists gave us a little money from time to time. But their people were poor too, so they could afford little. Mainly they provided volunteer help to serve and deliver meals."

"How are you supported now?"

"Mostly by private donations. We got a storefront at the edge of downtown from an old five and dime that went bankrupt. It was give it away or tear it down. It was cheaper for them to give it away. That helped somehow with their taxes. My wife does most of the cooking and we have some volunteer help. Not as much as we had before. If we had more resources, we could do more. Our building is beginning to deteriorate."

Thought turned upon thought in Hickey's head.

"Why do you do what you do, Captain Pearce?"

"The Lord has called Christians to live lives of gratitude for their salvation, Mr. Bishop. Thus I am called to serve him by serving those in need. The Lord calls us to care for those who can't care for themselves.

It's all in the twenty-fifth chapter of Matthew's Gospel. Do you have a Bible, Mr. Bishop?"

"Edward has a big old black Bible, Cap'n Pearce," Albert interjected, "and he reads it ever' day. He's a good Christian man when he's sober." Hickey glanced at him with a frown.

"I'd like the privilege of helping you remain a sober Christian, Mr. Bishop," Captain Pearce said, rising from his chair. "It's getting late, I should be getting back."

"Please return, Captain Pearce. I'd like to talk with you more. You may help my Christianity flourish more than you can possibly comprehend."

At that his guests excused themselves and Hickey stretched out on his couch in thoughtful contemplation.

CHAPTER TWENTY

The Fourth of July

Meanwhile, the summer was passing without incident, until the Fourth of July, that is. Hickey had remained sober, resisting strong temptation on two occasions, one being a dreary day early in May when he had become depressed, along with everyone else, because the sun hadn't shone in more than three weeks, the other was Memorial Day when he expected Josie to come but she didn't because the bars were closed and she had to remain home with Cass and had forgotten to tell him.

In April, he had gone to Albert's shed in the middle of the night and had placed the cardboard sign on his cart, but early the next morning the sun came streaming through his window at dawn and in his exuberance, he ran out before Albert began his rounds and slipped it back behind the stud.

On Memorial Day when she failed to appear, he got upset and wanted to drink, but he had no whiskey. It struck him then that it might be a good idea to keep a store of it in the cabinet, so that night he slipped to Albert's shed, slipped the cardboard from behind the stud and laid it on the cart. He wrote a check and drafted a note for a case of whiskey and enclosed them in an envelope. The next afternoon he was properly stocked for any emergency.

She came to him six days each week right after Cass left for the Sepia and stayed until late in the afternoon. She loved to cook and he loved to eat, and it showed. He added pounds and inches faster than I've ever seen any man add pounds and inches. Every time we slipped up the embankment from the two-track to visit him, he had grown fatter. His pants, which used to ride at his waist, held up by suspenders, now rode below his belly, which his suspenders encircled on each side. His stomach bulged so he couldn't fasten the bottom buttons of his shirt. But she never abated in the cooking nor he in the eating. His stomach, it seemed, had become the trophy of their relationship.

Then came the Fourth of July. Though Cass knew the Sepia had to be closed on the national holiday, he hoped that by some fluke Mr. Giles might be there and let him in to sneak a quick beer or two. Since there was to be a parade along Pine Street that day, he suspected that Giles just might be downtown. Josie humored him, knowing it would be useless to do otherwise, and she let him go, knowing that he would be gone for about an hour and she might slip down the path for a brief visit with Hickey.

The Fourth of July

When Cass got to the Sepia, he, of course, found it closed and became angry, kicking at the door but hurting only his foot. So he turned around and headed slowly home, his unsatisfied hope driving him into a very bad mood. Halfway back he met Albert who was on his way downtown with his decorated cart to march with the firemen in the Fourth of July parade, proudly dressed in the Sunday suit Josie had made for him. Cass stepped off the sidewalk onto the street and blocked Albert's progress.

"Where you be goin', little Mr. Junkman in your fancy suit?"

"Good mornin', Cass, I'm marchin' in the p'rade. Where you goin?"

"I be goin' get in yo' face, little junkman. What you be doin' wif my woman? Nuffin in this worl' rile me like a man messin' wif my woman."

Albert didn't understand. "Miss Josie is a fine lady, Cass, a fine lady. Her heart is pure gold. Pure gold."

"You got the gold, Mr. Junkman, where you keep your gold? Where you keep your money?"

Albert giggled and held up his coin purse. Cass came around the side of the cart to get a closer look. Albert opened it and showed Cass his coins. "I got... let me see..." he said, holding the purse close to his good eye and moving the coins around with his straight finger, "let me see... fifty... seventy-five... eighty-five... ninety... one, two three, ninety –three cents. I guess I'm pretty rich, ain't I?"

"No, the big money little junkman, the big money. Where you keep yo' big money?"

"I got six dollar home in a cigar box," Albert offered.

"They say you be rich, maybe a thousand, maybe a million. Where you stash your big money?"

"All I got is six dollar and... ninety-three cents."

"You lie!" he began to shout. "I think you be the white man she workin' fo' and I think you be rich. Everbody say so. Why else you be wearin' my meetin' suit and sittin' on my back stoop drinkin' my ice tea? An' why else she be comin down the two-track ever evenin' totin' roastin' beef, taters and greens? Ain't no rich white folks live back Amity Street 'cept'n you. Nobody else be eatin' roastin' beef ever night. And how you done stole my suit?"

Albert began to protest the interrogation and the accusations to the extent he understood them. He tried nervously to advance, but Cass, becoming aggressive, stepped between Albert and his pushcart and blocked his way.

"And you know what else, little Mr. Junkman wif the fancy suit? I think you be doin' my woman. Why else she be sleepin' on the couch nowadays? Why else, huh?" He was now loud and belligerent.

Albert, terrified, tried to move around Cass and back to his pushcart, but Cass grabbed him by the lapels of his suit. "You ain't goin' nowhere, little Mr. Junkman until you answer my questions!"

Albert backed away, turned and tried to run. Cass grabbed him from behind, swung him around and hit him in the stomach with his fist. When Albert doubled up in pain, with a quick upward jerk of his leg Cass kneed him in the face and smashed his nose. Blood spurting from his nostrils, Albert went down in a heap. Cass bent over and picked up the coin purse just as a police car providentially, but a minute too late, appeared and stopped. The officer chased and caught Cass and handcuffed him, then radioed for an ambulance. The ambulance took Albert to the hospital while the police car took Cass to jail.

The doctors and nurses at the hospital tended Albert as though he were a prince. He was a legend in the community, and everyone, including the wealthy, admired him, though few had ever done much to help him. They stopped the bleeding, packed gauze up his nostrils, cleaned him up and gave him a shot and a paper bag containing a bottle of pain pills, a bottle of antiseptic, a package of swabs and a set of written instructions for dressing the wounds. Then they called the fire chief from Number Two Station to take him home.

Late in the afternoon, Otis Blake, the fire chief brought Albert home in his red Ford pickup truck, still decorated for the parade, pushcart in the rear. Hickey and Mr. Benton happened to be standing together in the driveway, talking. Neither of them suspected that anything was amiss and both were shocked at what they saw. Albert, wincing in pain, was staggering toward his door on Otis's arm, nose bandaged, lips puffed, and eyes swollen and black. When he saw Hickey and Mr. Benton he mumbled, "He didn't mean nothin', he wasn't himself, he was all fretty. He thinks I stole his suit."

"Who? Who? Who did this to you? Was it Casien who hurt you?" Hickey demanded.

"Yeah, Cass done it, but he was all mixed up. Maybe he was drinkin'."

Hickey and Mr. Benton helped Otis walk Albert into his house and make him comfortable on the couch. Otis then handed Mr. Benton the sack containing the medical supplies. "This got pain pills and stuff in it," he said. "He's already had a shot and should be good for several hours. But before he goes to bed tonight, he ought to take one or two of these." After Mr. Benton assured him that he would care for Albert, Otis stepped outside and beckoned him and Hickey to follow.

"I'll tell you guys what the police told me," he said. "Just as a squad car rounded the corner of Amity and Walton, the officer saw Cass hit Albert in the stomach with his fist then knee him in the face. When Albert went down, the officer saw Cass pick up Albert's purse and run. The officer ran after him and caught him red handed stealing Albert's money, then he called for an ambulance. Poor old sot," he added with a quick glance at Hickey, "couldn't buy a beer today anyhow, being it's a holiday. Don't know why he done it. Albert didn't have no money to speak of. Anyway, they got Cass in jail and I don't know when they'll let him out."

When Mr. Benton assured Otis that Albert was in good hands, the chief, with Mr. Benton's help, unloaded Albert's cart and pushed it to the shed. Then Otis retrieved Albert's bloodied suit coat from seat of the truck and drove away.

"This baffles me, Edward," Mr. Benton said. "I can't understand why he would do such a thing. Cass ain't a violent man, even when he's drunk. And he should know the Sepia ain't open on the Fourth. I don't understand it." They went back inside, but Albert was asleep in his underwear, having removed his shirt and trousers. Hickey hanged Albert's suit coat on a peg.

"Mr. Benton, this is Albert's only suit, now it is dirty and crusted with blood. If I give you sufficient funds, would you be so kind as to take it to the drycleaner for him?" Mr. Benton consented, bundled up the suit, and left for home.

After Mr. Benton went home, Hickey went to get Josie, who was pacing from the front of her house to the back, wondering what had become of Cass. Hickey told her the whole story as they walked the two-track back to Hickey's house. When they arrived, Josie insisted on going directly to Albert's.

They went in quietly and stood over him. Josie began to cry. "Why he done this, Edward? Why he done this? Mr. Albert never hurt nobody. He never hurt Casien. Why he done this to my baby?" she said again as she ran her fingers over the blood stains on his shirt. "Where his suit I made him?"

"Mr. Benton will take it to the cleaners. Albert said it was all a misunderstanding, that Casien thought he stole his suit."

"That not so," she declared with certainty. Casien know Mr. Albert didn't steal his suit. Casien all messed up because I don't be sleepin' with him no more. He 'cuse me of 'ho'in'. Ever since Mr. Albert come to our house and drink ice tea, Casien think Mr. Albert be my new man. Then he get mad at me, and he slap me once when he be drunk. I don't know what to do Edward. I can't keep up like this."

They sat together by Albert's side until almost midnight, when Albert awoke. Then Josie carefully removed the old gauze and swabbed Albert's nostrils with the antiseptic, repacked them and put a new bandage over his nose while Albert fought pain and tears.

"What they going to do with Cass?" Albert asked, once he was comfortable. "He won't do this no more. Cass is okay. He was just mixed up. I think maybe he was drinking. Maybe he needed money to get more beer. He can have my six dollars in the cigar box. He thinks I stole his suit. Did you tell him we bought it, Edward? We didn't steal it, did we? He got mad when he seen me wearin' his suit. Let's just give him six dollars."

Josie and Hickey assured him that they had not stolen Cass's suit, though they were unsure of whether they had or not, and the reality of it began to trouble them. They gave Albert two of the pain pills and Albert changed into his pajamas and was soon asleep again, this time in his bed.

"Why don't you stay with me tonight?" Hickey suggested.

"No!" she declared vehemently, "not tonight. If Casien goin' 'cuse me of sleeping with Mr. Albert, by God, I make him to tell the truth. I stay here tonight and sleep on Mr. Albert couch and look after him. You just go home," and she clenched her lips in anger.

Hickey left and Josie stood over Albert as he slept in his little bed. She stroked his mussed up hair and whispered, "You jus' be my little baby, my little baby." Then she spent the night sleeping fitfully on Albert's couch, waking frequently.

Albert slept fitfully too, but did not awaken until sunup. When he awoke, he was surprised to find Josie still there. "You are good to me, Miss Josie," he declared with obvious appreciation, but speaking with great discomfort.

"You need to be took care of, and I be the one to do it, Mr. Albert. I be the one to do it. I be like yo' mama to you."

Again she redressed his wounded nose and brought him to the couch. "Would you like some breakfast," she asked.

"No, I ain't hungry. Do we got any coffee?"

"I make some," she said. "I make some at Mr. Edward's. I be back soon."

She went next door and found Hickey still asleep in the bed, but he awoke when he heard the coffee perking and smelled it's aroma. When it was finished, she poured him a cup and carried to pot to Albert's. He took a cup, thanked her, and settled into a comfortable position on the couch. When she was satisfied that he could be left alone for a time, she returned to Hickey's and took a long nap on his couch while he sat at the table, reading, writing and drinking coffee.

When Josie awoke late that morning she found Hickey asleep in his chair on the porch. She walked to Albert's, and found him asleep on his couch. Confusion set in. Two of her men asleep and the other in jail. She felt alone. Without knowing why, she took a fifth of whiskey from Hickey's case, put it into her picnic basket and headed down the two-track to her home on Wood Street.

CHAPTER TWENTY-ONE

You Ain't No Man!

When she got home, she was shocked to find Cass there, drunk but not as drunk as usual. "How you get out of jail?" she demanded.

"Ole Mr. Gile at the Sepia done bail me out," he said with a laugh. "The polices come to him this mornin' and tole him not to look for me on account I be in jail. Then Mr. Gile' come over and bail me. Say I be too good a customer to spend the day in jail when I should be in his place drinkin'. Then he take me to the Sepia for a few beers. Then he brung me home in his car. Just got here a minute ago. Where you been?"

Without answering she said, "Here, I brung you this," taking the bottle of whiskey from her basket and setting it firmly on the kitchen table.

"Where you get the whiskey?" he asked in a suspicious tone.

"Never you mine. I jus' got it. And you drink it if you want to."

He pried the cork out and took a long pull straight from the bottle, wiped his mouth on his shirt sleeve, then he set it down, imitating the firmness with which she had set the bottle on the table.

"You get this whiskey from yo' junkman?" he demanded.

"What you done to po' Mr. Bosch? Why you hurt him?" she screamed, ignoring his question.

"That little white trash junkman wearin' my meetin' suit, sittin' on my back stoop drinkin my ice tea and messin wif my woman. He be up for whuppin'."

"He just a poor ole man, and you be a damn fool!" she screamed. "You ain't no man, you just a damn old dumb fool!"

"He ain't no po' old man. You know it and I know it. He a rich junk man and you be his 'ho." He lurched toward her and swung and hit her in the ribs with his fist. As she staggered sideways he reached out and grabbed her arm. She tried to pull away but he slapped her across the face. "You be a 'ho!" he screamed, "You be a white man's 'ho!"

Anger and resentment welled up within her like she had never felt before. "An' what 'ho fetch you yo' supper ever night an' what 'ho give you money for drinkin' an' what 'ho pay fo' yo' taxi an' what 'ho pay fo' yo' rent? Huh? What 'ho do that fo' you? Huh? You the dumbest man I ever know!" she screamed, and she slammed the door and stomped toward the street.

She didn't go toward Hickey's down the two-track, instead she walked north on Wood Street, across the wooden sidewalk that spanned the swamp and the creek, and strode resolutely deep into the Negro section in an effort to walk off her anger. But the more she walked the more she thought, and the angrier she got. She walked on and on, heading first toward downtown, then curling around and winding her way east on the far side of the celery flats toward Hackley Motor Works. She walked and walked, and she thought and thought.

Finally, well after darkness had set in, she arrived at the two-track from the Getty Street side and walked back toward home. She first looked in on Albert and found him standing at his sink by the mirror, looking at his face and touching his swollen eyes. Without a word she redressed his injury. Then she went around the back to Hickey's and found him drinking.

He was shocked to see her. "I'm so sorry, my dear Josie, I thought you would not be back this evening." He pulled her to himself. She pulled away.

"I'm sorry, Josie. I can't be patronizing to Casien anymore. I hope they put him away for life. Better yet, I hope they give him the electric chair."

"He home and he drunk." she said tersely. "You eat yet?"

"No, I've had nothing."

Without a word she went to the icebox and selected some pieces of roast beef, put them in a pan, added a little catsup and stirred up some barbeque. She made two sandwiches and put them on plates.

"Here a sammish for you, and one for Mr. Albert," she said when she finished. "You take it over to him and keep him some company for a while. He be feelin' bad. You quit drinkin' and look after Mr. Albert. I be back tomorrow." Without another word she left for home, walking down the two-track.

Hickey took one more long pull from the bottle he had started, corked it and put it back in the cabinet, vowing not to touch it again that night. He walked over to Albert's, and they sat together and ate their sandwiches as the moon rose and shone in Albert's kitchen window.

They talked little, Albert finding expression painful, and Hickey having little to say. Both were deep in thought and feeling, and just quietly kept each other company until bedtime.

Late that night, Hickey gave Albert two more pills, waited until he was asleep, and went home and went to bed. He wanted to drink, but sense won out over compulsion, and he went to bed mostly sober, but slept poorly.

CHAPTER TWENTY-TWO

Serves Him Right!

Just as the early morning July sun rose above Albert's rooftop and streamed into his east window, Hickey awoke to the sound of fire engines, the acrid smell of smoke and a banging on his door. Josie was there, crying and trembling, arms full of things she'd brought from home.

"Let me in," she cried. And he saw her face, stained with tears, her eyes swollen and her usually neat hair a gnarled mess. She was carrying her picnic basket and a bulging battered valise. He looked westward over her head and saw tall tongues of flames and billowing black smoke roaring high above the tree line in the direction of her house. Just then he heard a loud crunching noise and huge, violent clouds of sparks leaped skyward. He pulled her in and closed the door.

"You got what you want," she blurted out. "He dead. I done it. I shoot him. I shoot him and I light the house on fire."

"Josie," he said, weakly, trembling.

"Shhh." she said. "Can't nobody know I here."

"What did you do?" he asked, helping her unload her cargo onto the table.

"I give him some of your whiskey yesterday and he drunk most of it down. Then he said nasty things and got mad and hit me," she said, raising her sleeve and showing him a swollen bruise on her arm where he had grabbed her. "Then he cuss some more and I take a long walk all around and around and all the way back to Getty. Then I come here down the two-track and make you and Mr. Albert a sammish.

"When I get back I find him pass out on the floor, done drunk most of your bottle of whiskey. He be pass out. I sit by him on the floor for a long time and get madder and madder. Cryin'. I be mad and sad at the same time. You want him dead and he is dead but he ain't dead. And I think he ought to be dead cuz he ain't got no life left. And I ain't got no life left if I stay with a dead man. So I find his gun in the closet and I shoot him in the head. I pack my belongins and sit by him all night, and jus' as the sun peek up I tip over the kerosene heater, light the place on fire and take off out the back door. It be finish."

Hickey was stunned. "Oh, dear Josie," he whispered as he held her. Then his mind began to work. "Did anyone see you?"

"No. Nobody see me."

"You'll stay here now. You are safe with me."

"But they be lookin' for me."

"Let's just wait and see what develops."

"Here the gun," she said, reaching into her basket and removing Cass's old baseball cap with a very small twenty-two caliber pistol nestled inside. "It be Casien's. He say he need it for pertection." She cried. "But he don't need no pertection no more."

Hickey took the hat containing the gun from her outstretched hand. "I'll be right back," he said. Then he stepped outside. He returned in less than a minute, without the gun.

He held her as she cried. "I got just you now Edward," she said trembling, "just you...." Then she added, "Maybe that good."

"We've got each other, Dear Josie. We've got each other." As she sobbed he mumbled, "for better or for worse... in sickness and in health...

until death us do part.... By the power vested in me...." He trailed off.

She smiled through her tears and hugged him tightly.

They spent the rest of the morning together, doing little. She stayed in the house, away from the door and out of sight, occasionally peering out the window to the west. By noon the air had cleared but the pungent smell of fire pervaded the whole neighborhood.

Hickey looked in on Albert. Albert felt a little better after a good night's sleep. His swelling had subsided somewhat. Hickey didn't tell Albert what had happened. Shortly after noon, while he was still at Albert's, the iceman came.

"What's the ruckus down the street?" Hickey asked innocently, stepping out the back door and meeting him at his truck.

"Old Cass White's house burned down this morning. He was in it. Body was burned pretty bad but there was no mistakin' his busted head. That's what Otis said. Serves him right for what he done to Albert."

"Yes it seems it does. Albert is in severe pain. Do you have any ice chips?"

The iceman carried the block of ice into the house and put it in the icebox. Then he saw Albert. "That damn drunk made a mess out of you all right. The cop at the fire told me. He got what he had comin' to him." He gave Hickey a small scoop of ice chips that he scraped up from the back of his truck. Hickey poured an old sock full and told Albert to lie back on his bed with the ice pack on his eyes and nose. It felt soothing.

"What happened?" Albert asked.

"Cass's house burned down this morning with him in it," the iceman explained, breaking the news to Albert rather bluntly. "Some fire," he said. "Mighty hot. Melted the flesh right off'n his bones. He's half cremated already," he laughed. "There won't be much left for the undertaker to do. He sure had it comin'."

"Was Cass drunk when he died?" asked Albert.

"Probably," answered the ice man, "Probably he was dead drunk. Had an empty whiskey bottle right next to him. Probably never knew what happened. That's what Otis said."

"Leave me an extra block of ice, please," Hickey instructed the ice man. He brought another block down and set it on the carpet by Albert's stoop. Then he backed out the drive and continued his rounds.

"Did Cass go to heaven?" Albert asked Hickey after the ice man had left.

"That's for God to decide," Hickey answered. "He knows the heart of man."

"Is Miss Josie okay?"

"Yes, Miss Josie is fine."

"Where she going to live?"

"She'll be staying with me."

"That's good. I'd miss her if she went away."

Hickey made sure Albert was comfortable before going back home.

CHAPTER TWENTY-THREE

Your Fellow Drunkard

Hickey and Josie remained in the house the rest of the day, being very quiet. He ventured out twice to check on Albert, who was beginning to feel some better.

About five o'clock the paperboy slipped the *Chronicle* through the mail slot. They paged through it together on the table until they found the story on the last page of the local news section. The one column headline read *Man Dies in House Fire*. He read her the story aloud:

Casien (Cass) White, a local Negro, perished this morning when his home on Wood Street was destroyed by fire. He was believed to have been about forty. Otis Blake, Hackley fire chief, declared the fire to have been caused by the accidental upsetting of a kerosene heater coupled with excessive drinking. An empty whiskey bottle next to the body had led investigators to conclude that White was intoxicated at the time of the fire.

White is reported by police to have assaulted well known Hackley trash collector, Albert Bosch, during an altercation on the Fourth of July, and neighbors say he argued vehemently with his common law wife, a mulatto known only as Queen Anne, after coming home drunk yesterday. Neighbors said that she left him after the argument, possibly motivating him to drink heavily through the night.

White is best remembered by the residents of Hackley's east side as a once-promising baseball player who played briefly in the Negro League but who apparently took to drink after being injured in a brawl in a Negro nightclub in Memphis. Officials have declared the fire and death to have been accidental and have closed the case. The body was interred in the cemetery behind the County Poor Farm.

She sat quietly for a long time. "Do that mean we free?" she finally asked.

"Yes my dear, we are free. But I think it best if we keep to ourselves and live very quietly for a time. Let us have a little drink to quiet our nerves."

"I drink a little tea," she answered. "I won't never drink none of that whiskey."

He poured her a glass of tea and himself a glass of whiskey. They sipped slowly, and sat together on the couch for a long time, saying nothing.

"Edward, I shoot him in the head, right in the dent where the ball hit him. The bullet finish what the ball start. Do I be a murderer? I think really the ball kill him. He die a long time ago." She was still sobbing quietly.

"No my dear, you only executed God's judgment on him for his sin, just as the ancient Israelites wrought God's judgment upon the pagan Canaanites for their abominations." he said, pouring himself another drink. "No, my dear Josie, you are innocent. You are the Lord's arm of justice. I doubt if he would ever have been punished for what he did to poor Albert, justice being what it is these days."

"But I feel like I murder him," she sobbed.

"Don't feel that way," he admonished.

"But I can't help how I feel." He poured another glass of whiskey. "Sometimes I think I do him a good thing so he don't have to live like this no more. Sometimes I think I be playin' God and disobeyin' the Commands. Sometimes I think I be the selfishest person in the world. Did he go to heaven, Edward? Did he go to heaven?"

"That's God's judgment," he answered. "It's none of our business. Do you want to see him when you get there? I think for me heaven would be happier without him. If the fire wasn't enough hell for him, maybe God...."

He left his thought unfinished.

"I think you orta stop drinkin' for tonight," she said. "You startin' to get nasty and talk like a bad man. I don't like it when you nasty. Besides, it not smart to get drunk. Maybe the polices come to find me."

"Alright, you win, dear. You are right, of course. I repent. I apologize for my ill-conceived, unchristian comments. I should never have said such things. I should never have thought such things. I think I'll go look in on Albert," he said, and corking his bottle got up and left, a little wobbly.

Albert had just awakened and was sitting up in a chair by the table. Hickey pulled up a chair across from him and they began to talk, Albert explaining that he was feeling better, but that he wanted to take another pill before going to bed. Just as Hickey was pumping water for him, a car pulled up in the drive next to Albert's house. Hickey froze, thinking it may be the police.

It was not a police car, but an ordinary sedan, a handsome black Buick. The door opened and Dominie VandeBruin got out.

"Mr. Bosch, are you home?" he shouted, peering through the screen door.

"Yes, Domie Vannerbine, come in," Albert answered before Hickey could object. As he entered the room Hickey stepped back into the far corner, and, seeing only Albert in the dim light, the dominie extended his hand.

"Mr. Bosch, we heard what happened to you, and we're terribly sorry. How are you feeling?" he asked, facing Albert with his back to Hickey, who blended into the shadows of the darkened room.

"I'm mendin', Domie," Albert answered.

"I guess God executed swift punishment on that drunkard, Cass White, did he not?" he asserted with a broad smile.

"Oh, Cass, he just got mixed up. He thought I stole his suit," Albert responded. "Yes, Cass got brent up. He drank, but he wasn't so bad. I knew him for a long time. He was a good ball player once, but he got hurt and he couldn't play no more. That broke his heart and he took to drink. But he wasn't a bad man. He teaches the young boys how to play as good as him. He was just mixed up. Did he go to heaven, domie?"

"Of course not. There are no drunkards in heaven. Paul said so. And we are not to associate with them.

"Mr. Bosch," he said, suddenly straightening up and beginning to look around, "do I detect the odor of spirits in your house? Have you been drinking?"

"No, Domie Vannerbine, I don't...." But before Albert could finish his sentence, VandeBruin, looking around, spotted Hickey standing by the pump.

"Mr. ...ah   Hickey Bishop, is that you?" he asked, seeing Hickey for the first time since their days together at the seminary, but without a spark of recognition.

"Yes, Dominie, it is I," Hickey answered, looking the dominie straight in the eye and clearly recognizing his former student, now a little heavier, a little older, and a little and sterner of countenance. A cloud of sadness enveloped him.

"Hickey Bishop, do you know the awful judgment God has wrought upon your fellow drunkard, Cass White?" Hickey nodded that he knew. "That could be the judgment God will mete out to you if you don't repent." Then turning to Albert he added, "Mr. Bosch, you should not keep company with drunkards. The evil spirit that inhabits him may reach out and claim you as its next victim."

Albert, unable to protest or debate, kept silent. Hickey excused himself and went home to Josie. Dominie VandeBruin stayed for a short while reprimanding Albert further, and got into his car and left. About suppertime, Hickey brought over a plate of roast beef, potatoes and gravy. Albert picked at his food, set the plate aside and returned to his couch, confused, but convinced that the dominie was being unfair to his good neighbor.

CHAPTER TWENTY-FOUR

The Hore of Babbylin'

Back then it was the custom of the Dutch Church to conduct annual family visitations. The dominie and an elder would schedule visits to the homes of the parishioners. Together they would "inspect" the house, to see if there were any evidence of heresy or misbehavior and would, in my words, conduct an inquisition of the family members, including the children, to ascertain if each was "making his election sure."

Since Albert had indicated a wish to become communicant member of the church, the dominie scheduled him for visitation, but Albert forgot the time and date. That's how it happened that the dominie and Elder Doorn arrived one evening at seven a few days later just as Josie was at Albert's house dressing his wounds.

They watched as she carefully removed the bloody cotton from his nose, swabbed his nostrils and repacked them with fresh cotton, all the time reassuring him that his nose was looking better and apologizing for causing him any pain. After she taped a fresh bandage to his nose, she left.

"Who was that Negress?" the dominie wanted to know. "Is she a nurse from the poor farm?"

"She's Miss Josie, she's my neighbor," Albert answered.

"Your neighbor? Where does she live?"

"She lives in Mr. Bishop's house."

"What! Is he unequally yoked to a Colored woman?"

"She takes care of him… and me. She makes us our supper and washes our clothes, and cleans our houses. She is a good neighbor, and a good nurse. She takes good care of my broke nose."

"Are she and the drunkard married?"

"I don't think so. She was Cass's wife before."

"I thought she looked familiar," the elder interjected. "But I ain't seen her in a long time."

"She was married to the other drunkard?" the dominie asked. "Do she and Drunkard Bishop now share a bed?"

"I don't know. They ain't got but one."

The dominie sat down at the table, clasped his hands together and spoke very seriously. "Mr. Bosch," he pontificated, "That woman is a harlot and Hickey Bishop is a drunkard, an adulterer and a whoremonger."

"Mr. Bishop's name is Edward, not Hickey. Only people who make fun at him call him that," Albert declared, boldly coming to his neighbor's rescue.

"He does drink heavily, does he not?" VandeBruin asked, ignoring Albert's admonition.

"Yes, he drinks sometime to forget his miseries."

"And I'm told by quite a reliable source that when he drinks he curses the church. Do you know that to be true?"

"Oh no domie, he don't curse the church. He curse the evil in the church. He says the church been seducted by the hore of Babbylin."

"He should know all about whores," the dominie declared.

"And about being 'seducted'," the elder added with a half grin.

"Adulterers, whoremongers, harlots and drunkards deserve no respect from anyone," the dominie declared, vehemently, "the Lord will have nothing to do with them. They are possessed by evil demons, and it behooves the elect to stay as far from them as possible too. At any time, without warning, the demons may come out of them and get into someone else, as they did with the swine in Jesus' day. You wouldn't want that, now would you? For your own good, you should stay away from them!"

"No. I don't want no evil spirit coming in me," Albert confessed. "But I don't know if Edward and Miss Josie are evil. They don't seem evil. Edward says that King Sollyman said it was okay for people to drink whiskey if they are perishing."

"How could a drunkard know what Solomon said?"

"Edward reads the Bible. And I read the Proverbs too. I know he said that."

"Even Satan knows and can quote the scriptures!"

"But they are my good neighbors," Albert responded, wringing his hands in obvious distress, and becoming eloquent in spite of his speech impediment. "We all help each other. We need each other. We ain't got nobody else to take care of us. Edward says that we are called to be our brother's keeper."

"How can you call a drunkard and a whoremonger your brother?" the dominie demanded to know.

"I ain't got no live brothers. Edward says we are brothers 'cause we take care of each other, and Miss Josie, Miss Josie is not evil." And getting his courage up added, "She is a blessted lady."

"Mr. Bosch," Elder Doorn chimed in, "as long as you keep company with harlots and drunkards, you cannot become a communicant member of the body of Christ. Our Lord would not stand for it and neither can we. Our duty is to protect the Lord's Supper from pollution by dirty hands, you understand, and you befoul your hands by the evil company you keep."

The dominie rose from his chair and walked toward the door. "You may continue to visit the church and sit in the back row, Mr. Bosch. We will allow that with the hope that by hearing the Word of God preached you may repent and reject your evil companions. And we shall also expect you to tithe. The Lord commands us to tithe, you know. Let's begin by seeing if you can be obedient in small things."

With that they wiped their feet on Albert's welcome mat and left his house.

The next evening at supper, Albert, Edward and Josie discussed the dominie's visit. As Albert explained that "Domie Vannerbine" told him he shouldn't be keeping company with "drunkers, 'dulters, harlots and horsmunkers," because they couldn't get in heaven and because they were "full of evil spirits what might get loose and get into him." Hickey grew uneasy and began to pace the floor around the table. Josie looked at him with a worried look on her face.

"Do you think we're evil, Albert?" Hickey asked.

"Domie Vannerbine says so, and he knows the Bible like you do Edward. Everybody's talk just mixes me all up. I don't know what to think. You and him read the same Bible but you say different things. You are my friend, my brother, and he is the domie. He preaches to me, but we take care of each other. I don't know what I would do without you and Miss Josie now."

"And we need you too, Albert, my dear brother. We need you too." And Josie nodded in assent.

"Maybe I shouldn't go to church no more," Albert said, more with the inflection of a question than a statement.

"No, Albert, do as the dominie says. Just sit in the back row and listen to the preaching of the Word. Dominie VandeBruin knows the Word and preaches it well. Our discussions of his sermons edify me," he said, reflecting on the days at seminary when he taught the dominie the art of preaching and the interpretation of the scriptures. His discussions of the dominie's sermons were his only solid connection with his happy past.

"And he said I'm s'posed to tithe. What's tithe, Edward?"

"The Lord asks us to return to him a tenth of what we receive at his hand. For every dollar you earn, you should place ten cents on the offering plate. And a dollar of each ten, for example. I agree that you should tithe. We all are called upon to tithe. If you would like, I could help you each week determine what your tithe should be."

"I would like that, Edward. I want to do what God says. Do you tithe, Edward?"

"Yes, I do, Albert. I don't place my tithe in the offering plate, I contribute it covertly to the seminary under my prior identity, but I'm thinking of changing that. I'm learning that there are other worthy causes in the world in which we are to serve as priests. I think my money could serve the Lord better elsewhere. I think you should go home now, Albert, I'm feeling rather upset."

"Okay," said Albert, "I feel lots better now. I think I go back to work in the morning. I gotta earn money if I'm gonna tithe."

CHAPTER TWENTY-FIVE

Like the 'Postle Paul

The next morning when Albert took his cart from the shed, the cardboard was lying face up. Dutifully, Albert procured the whiskey from Petrone's and delivered it to Hickey. Hickey spent the next four days drunk while Josie stayed with him pondering their condition. But this time it was different. Hickey didn't stagger around, kick things and scream scathing disparagement as before, rather this time he staggered slowly and carried on a somewhat incoherent dialog with himself regarding matters of the faith. Though his words made little sense to us who listened, he seemed lucid to himself.

When he was drinking, we stayed out of his way. Often we just lay on the cool grassy bank below the two-track listening to him debate with himself the meaning of godliness, or watching the older boys working bareback in the celery fields below, weeding or carrying and stacking the bleaching boards, thankful that we didn't have to go to work until next summer and enjoying the last bit of childhood we had left.

Sometimes on Saturday afternoon we walked back on the two-track and went to visit Hickey, Josie and Albert. We had come to the conclusion that Albert was not rich, but we had no idea how Hickey and Josie were able to eat so well and how he was able drink so much. Our parents were able to afford roast beef only on Sunday, but they seemed to eat it every day of the week. The junk business couldn't be that lucrative.

The Bakers knew that Hickey drank a lot now because they could hear him talking to himself in the back yard, and they said they couldn't understand how he provided for himself. They suggested he be investigated for having no visible means of support, but the police said they couldn't investigate him until he committed some crime, and being drunk in his own back yard was not a crime, even though the Bakers and Dominie VandeBruin thought it was. The police were not Dutch.

Though he drank heavily during the week, Hickey did not drink on Sundays. He insisted on keeping the Sabbath day holy. He and Josie would rise late, often after church had begun, and begin preparing dinner. It was difficult for them because he was terribly hung over and usually had the shakes. So on Sunday morning they each stayed out of the other's way, he trying to read or write and she puttering in the kitchen. But by noon they were on their best behavior for Albert.

Albert continued to go to church every Sunday and sit in the back row. At noon he had his usual nice dinner with Hickey and Josie and reported on the sermon and the prayer. Hickey's interest in hearing all about church and the dominie never waned. Even though his drinking increased, and even though from the pulpit the dominie condemned him for his drunkenness, Hickey never spoke a bad word in return. Except for the dominie's admonition to stay away from him, he encouraged Albert to listen carefully and abide by his words.

"Do you think I'm an evil man, Albert?" he asked one day in early August, as he often did.

"No, Edward, you are a good man. You just got this thorn in your flesh, like the 'Postle Paul."

"You are a true friend, Albert, a true friend. I am blessed to have you as my friend and neighbor. You are a prince of a man."

"I am blessted to have you too, Edward."

"Albert, I'd like to talk with Captain Pearce. When you make your rounds tomorrow, would you be so kind as to mention to the Captain that I'd like to see him?"

"Yes, I will. He asks about you every time I see him."

"That's nice to know. I think he and I might be able to help each other."

On Monday afternoon, immediately after Albert stopped at Soldiers of the Cross, Captain Pearce drove to Hickey's house and knocked on the front door. "Come around the back, around Albert's place," Hickey shouted after looking out the front window and seeing Pearce's car, "the front door won't open."

The Captain ran quickly around Albert's house to Hickey's back door. "Are you feeling under compulsion?" the Captain asked, breathlessly.

"Oh, no. I'm fine," Hickey answered. "I want to discuss with you a matter of mutual interest. Could Soldiers of the Cross sponsor a team in the Veterans' Association Youth League, if it had the money, that is?"

"I don't know," he answered, after a thoughtful pause, "we've never considered such a thing. Our money goes to feed the hungry, not promote athletics. We aren't even able to serve the needy as we should."

"Well, I know of some boys who are needy, and maybe need goes beyond the stomach. I know of some boys who need a baseball team."

"I'm sure there are boys who do, but we can't justify using our meager funds to sponsor a baseball team as long as children are going to bed hungry at night."

"Would it be possible for me to provide you with an endowment, one that would substantially increase your ability to serve the needy, and yet designate certain funds for a particular use?"

"What do you have in mind?" he asked, with a skeptical look in his eye.

"Captain," he continued, taking a deep breath and adding a tone of authority to his voice, "The Lord has blessed me with resources that are not evidenced by my material surroundings. I'd like to direct some of those resources to certain specific causes."

"Are you being honest with me, Mr. Bishop? You've not been drinking?"

"I'm perfectly sober, Captain, perfectly sober. You'll have to trust me."

"I'm listening," he answered, torn between skepticism, belief and indulgence.

"To begin, I'd like you to sponsor a baseball team in the Veterans' Association Youth League, beginning next season. I'll provide an endowment sufficient to purchase shirts, caps and other equipment, and cover the cost of maintaining the team from year to year. The shirts will have Soldiers of the Cross written on the front, along with a number on the back. Mr. Benton will assist you in the process of establishing the team and securing a coach, the clothing and other materials. And, by the way, it will be a team of Colored boys."

"I've often hoped that the boys from the Negro District could field a team," he responded. "I've felt badly for them. Used to play a little ball myself," he added with a smile that failed to conceal a touch of pride. "I'd be grateful for the opportunity to help them," he responded, Hickey's tone of authority dispelling his skepticism.

"There's more." Hickey said. "One condition of the endowment will be the continuing sponsorship of the team. A second clause will provide substantial continuing support for your charitable programs. And I do mean substantial. I, too, abhor hunger. I am also in the process of drafting a will and establishing a trust to provide for Mr. Bosch and Miss LaFarge in the event they survive me. I have the entire plan down on paper. I hope you would be so kind as to take it to attorney Jacob Hekkema for formal drafting. He has consented to be the executor for the endowment and for my will."

Captain Pearce stood in stunned silence.

"There's still more," Hickey said. "I've been reading about the city wanting to sell the property on which the school once stood, but are unable to find a buyer. I've never seen a price. How much are they asking, do you have any idea?"

"I think they'd let the whole block go for under two thousand, maybe just one, I don't know. The neighborhood is going downhill, you know. Why, what are you thinking?"

"I'd like to give Soldiers of the Cross the money to buy the block, build themselves a suitable building, and develop a proper baseball field.

A real proper baseball field. Your organization would own and manage it, and the endowment would cover the cost of construction and maintenance far into the future. Attorney Hekkema will negotiate the purchase of the property."

"That block is big enough for a building and for four fields," the Captain exclaimed, "with backstops back to back in the middle and diamonds reaching out toward the four corners," he added excitedly. "The whole league could play there. We could erect fences all around, and even have bleachers. We could run water and have drinking fountains and restrooms!"

"I appreciate your exuberance, Captain. I am equally thrilled. There is a consideration. I will insist that the field be named the *Casien White Memorial Field,* and that the new building that houses the Soldiers of the Cross be named in memory of Mr. Bosch, after he passes from this life. I will also insist that my financial participation remain totally confidential."

An ecstatic Captain Pearce stood in stunned silence, teetering between ecstasy and disbelief. "And just one other thing, Captain, since you are the beneficiary of a windfall, I'd like you to offer employment to Mr. Benton. The horse boarding business can no longer provide him with income sufficient to provide for his family and living costs are continually increasing. His little girl is bright and should have an education, preferably a Christian education. Mr. Benton is a very capable and dependable man, and I'm sure he can be extremely useful in many ways, particularly in the maintenance of properties. The man has the heart of Christ, but lacks understanding of scripture. I would hope that under your guidance he might come to a saving knowledge of the Lord."

The Captain nodded in grateful assent.

So, with that Hickey handed him the document and a check for more money than he had ever seen at one time, and Captain Pearce left with jaunty step, happier than he'd been for a long time. And so was Hickey.

CHAPTER TWENTY-SIX

A Proper Field

The rest of the summer slipped slowly by almost without incident. Albert recovered and continued making his rounds, but with less enthusiasm and vigor. Calvin and I spent the hot days swimming in the creek, spying on Hickey and Josie, searching for treasure in Albert's back yard, lying in wait hoping Audrey would come out naked again, or talking with Hickey and Josie when he was sober, which wasn't very often anymore. When he was drinking, she wouldn't let us talk to him.

Engines droned night and day at the Hackley Motor Works on the other side of the valley. We rode our bikes over there some times, but guards wouldn't let us past the front gate. Many of the Dutch men in our neighborhood worked there and said that they were making engines for tanks and bombers.

The war was on and we had invaded Normandy earlier in the summer. Sometimes olive drab Piper Cubs flew overhead and dropped leaflets urging us to turn in tin cans at the armory and to collect milkweed pods for making life vests for the sailors. Once a flying fortress flew so low over the celery flats that we could see the bombardier sitting in the nose of the plane. In the fields north of the plant they tested tanks. We climbed up on the fence and watched as the tanks rolled over the moguls or spun around on their tracks. We stayed and watched until the guards came around and chased us away.

Some of our friends' fathers were in the war and we prayed every night by our beds for our soldiers. Some of the men from our church were killed in action and every time one died, they would add his name to the big plaque that hung in the entrance. I had two uncles in the war and we had a little banner hanging in our living room window with two blue stars on it. When my Uncle Johnny was killed, they changed his star to gold.

As August wore on, Hickey drank more and more. But now his drinking seemed different. Hickey was no longer angry. The more he drank, the happier he became. We couldn't understand the transformation.

We read in the *Chronicle* that the city had sold the school yard to the Soldiers of the Cross and that they were developing it into real baseball diamonds for the Youth League.

Sometimes we would stand where the old backstop had stood, watching the work at the playfield. After Cass died nobody played ball there anymore and the place went to waste and weeds, but then one day dump trucks began bringing in dirt and a

A Proper Field

bulldozer smoothed it out. Workers made infields out of clay and planted grass seed in the outfields. They built four backstops in the middle and put up fences around the perimeter. Then they brought in bleachers. The *Chronicle* had a story and a new picture every few days.

On Labor Day morning they had a ceremony. Captain Pearce, Mr. Benton and even the mayor came and dedicated the field, putting up a sign that read, *Casien White Memorial Field*. Then they closed it for the rest of the year so the grass could grow.

On Labor Day afternoon we marched in the parade beside Albert. We didn't tease him any more. Hickey had asked us not to, and since Cass beat him up we didn't feel like it. Dominie VandeBruin told us that the fire at Cass's house was the beginning of his hell for having hurt Albert, and that it must have been the devil that prompted the Soldiers of the Cross to name the ball field in honor of a Negro drunkard.

We started school the day after Labor Day and being in the seventh grade, we had to go to a different building, the high school. It seemed ironic. We were no longer the oldest kids in our building, and though our childhood had, for all practical purposes, ended on Labor Day, the older students treated us like children because we were the youngest kids in our new school. But Calvin and I felt superior because we knew things that no one else knew, not even the adults.

Then the tragedy happened.

CHAPTER TWENTY-SEVEN

Alone of the Sidewalk

Late in October we had our first cold snap. The days had been in the eighties and the nights in the sixties, so no one started their furnaces. But one Saturday night the north wind began to blow and the temperature plunged unseasonably into the thirties.

In the morning, before church, the Dutch people all crawled out from under their thick quilts and fired up their coal furnaces, sending clouds of black smoke and soot shooting into the air to be blown about by the wind. It had not been that smoky in the neighborhood since Cass's fire. Albert, Hickey and Josie needed heat too.

They had not used their kerosene heaters since the spring, and they were completely dry. Mr. Benton went over to Albert's house that morning after Albert had left for church to get his fire started and warm up his house. When he went out back to fill Albert's kerosene can, he found Hickey at the barrel tapping a bucketful for himself, but having trouble getting the tap open, his hands were shaking so. He helped him fill his bucket and asked him if he wanted help getting his heater started. Hickey said no and he was shivering and acting grumpy, so Mr. Benton decided to leave him alone. Besides, Josie came out to the barrel to help him carry the kerosene bucket into the house. So he decided to steer clear of them and let them fend for themselves.

That morning Albert sat, as usual in the back row, happy to be where it was warm. On that cold Sunday morning Dominie VandeBruin preached at length about the fires of hell being hotter than the fires in our furnaces, and warning God's chosen people to live pious lives in order to make their election sure. At eleven o'clock he said amen. They sang their closing hymn and he gave the benediction.

Just as the ushers opened the church doors they heard the clanging of fire engines in the distance. Albert, as usual, was the first to step out of the door of the church. When he heard the crackling sound and saw the towering flames and billows of smoke rising to the sky over on Amity Street, he knew instantly that there would be no dinner that day.

Albert was among the first to leave the church but, because of his lame leg, was among the last to get to the fire. Calvin and I raced the three blocks to Amity Street and beat everyone except the best high school athletes in the church, Donny Eldersveld and Jelte Veenstra. Otis Blake had already pulled his red '39

Ford pickup, with its big chrome siren on the front fender, into Albert's driveway and the firemen were just connecting the hose from the pumper truck to the fireplug down on the corner. The hook 'n ladder from firehouse Number Two came clattering up last.

Hickey's house was totally engulfed in flames. Fire was pouring out from the eaves like a blowtorch, and flames were coming out all around the bottom of the house between the shingles and the concrete blocks. At both the front and back peaks where the vents were, the orange flames were shooting out, then upward, towering above the big old sugar maple.

I think the entire congregation gathered on Bomers's, Douma's and Van Laar's front porches across the street to watch long tongues of flames spiraling toward the sky. The bungalow remained recognizable for only a few moments after its roof began to sag, and before the firemen could even start their hoses, the roof collapsed, sending showers of sparks roaring up the shaft of heat and in a flash igniting the dry leaves still clinging to the old maple tree. Mr. Baker, who had run home from church, stood in his driveway squirting a meaningless stream of water from his garden hose, which turned to steam in the conflagration. As the walls collapsed inward, he was forced to retreat.

Fed by old dry wood and sizzling tar paper, flames more searing than I have ever felt flared skyward, and popped and sagged and snapped and belched as the firemen waited for the water to make its way from the hydrant to the pumper. "The fury of hell," I heard the dominie say as he came and stood next to me and

Calvin. On his face was a smile of contentment that I had only seen once before.

Finally the hose stiffened and bulged as the water arrived. Firemen with hoses stretching from the pumper poured water on Baker's house, which had already begun to blister from the heat, and they soaked the smoldering embers that had flown upward in the draft and floated downward on to Albert's roof. Otis Blake stood in front of us and barked orders through a megaphone. "Just save the neighbor's houses! Get that ember up there by the chimney!" he yelled to the man with the hose, and "Put them hedges out before the fire gets to Albert's house!" and, "Watch out for those branches coming down off the tree!"

When the heat and the fire finally began to subside, they turned their hoses on the inferno that had, just minutes before, been Hickey's house. With a roar the water exploded into steam as it collided with the swirling tempest of flame.

As the fire abated, the air cooled a bit and we edged our way off the porches down to the street near the fire engines. A small crowd had gathered around Mr. Benton, who was smudged and sweaty. "She yelled at me when the fire started. We tried to drag him out, but we couldn't," he said. "We'd pull him one way and he'd fall the other way. He must weigh more than three hundred pounds. He fell down and we couldn't move him. Then it got so hot and smoky that I couldn't see nothing no more. The smoke got in my eyes. My eyes was burnin' and I couldn't breathe. I felt like I was going to explode. I had to run. I pulled on her, but she wouldn't let go of him. She jerked herself loose of me. She was screaming. I don't know what she done. I think she was still trying to drag him out. I think maybe he got up and fell on top of her." Then after a long pause he added, "I knew something bad was going to happen when he staggered over to Albert's and got that pail of kerosene, all shaky and stinkin' and hung over. I knew he'd dump that stuff all over the place and set himself on fire. I just knew it. He wouldn't let me help. Now him and her is both dead."

When only a few hot spots remained, four rain coated firemen and Otis Blake, wearing his white helmet, sloshed through the smoldering ruins with spades and picks looking for the corpses. Finally, just as a black Cadillac hearse pulled up through the police barricade, one of them shouted and Otis walked toward him. The one who found the bodies brushed away a few sticks of smoking lumber with a spade and poked at the bloated heap of steaming flesh with the toe of his boot, while the other nodded, affirming positive identification.

Just then an official looking man wearing a black suit got out of the hearse and walked to the edge of the smoking ruins closest to the spot where the corpses lay. The man squatted and shielded his face with his hands and peered at the bodies. Then he straightened up and called out to Otis Blake. He came over and they talked briefly, nodded together in assent, and the man in the suit came back to his hearse, got in, and drove away. "That was Doctor Martin, the coroner.

He just pronounced them legally dead," declared Mrs. Bomers, stating for her own edification an obvious fact that everyone else already knew. "And he sure don't want to mess up his nice hearse with them stinkin' corpses."

We watched as the firemen retrieved a heavy canvas from the hook 'n ladder, drenched it with water, laid it next to the clump of indiscernible human flesh, and together, using spades and pick handles, rolled the charred, sizzling heap of remains onto the canvas and dragged it to the edge of the foundation. Otis backed his red Ford pickup into Baker's driveway and the four firemen, each at a corner of the canvas, clumsily hoisted their heavy load onto the bed of the truck, folded the canvas over the bodies and tucked the corners under so the wind wouldn't blow it open. They slammed the tailgate shut. Then the four firemen got into the truck, two in the front and two in the back with the cargo, and drove slowly out of Baker's drive hauling their freight eastward down Amity Street toward the edge of town.

Otis came over to talk to Mr. Benton. I edged my way through the crowd to hear what he had to say. "Looked like he was on top of her... like they was... you know.... We couldn't get them apart, like they had just melted together, fused into one lump of flesh. Strangest thing... out here all you can smell is the stink of burnin' tarpaper, but in there," he said, pointing to the place where the corpses had lain, "in there it smells like roastin' beef." And he shook his head and walked away.

The crowd began to disperse, the Dutch returning to their homes and their traditional dinner, just a little later than usual.

Otis Blake got behind the big wooden steering wheel at the back end of the hook 'n ladder and proudly helped steer it back toward the fire station.

Albert Bosch stood alone on the sidewalk crying, and no one paid any attention.

CHAPTER TWENTY-EIGHT

A Prince of a Man

Mr. Bomers, who lived directly across the street from Albert and Hickey, had a seat on the city council, so the mess was cleaned up promptly. City workers hauled away the ashes and debris, leveled and raked the ground, and cut down the charred old sugar maple that once shaded the homes of Hickey Bishop and Albert Bosch. The firemen from Number Two Station built a new tall wooden privacy fence on the edge of Albert's property to hide his collection of junk There was no news story, no obituary in the *Chronicle*, nothing to memorialize the deaths of Hickey and Josie except the items in the police and fire reports that a house had burned on Amity Street and that two occupants of uncertain identity had died. There were no memorial services, No one recorded the burial of either body, but the Dutch of Hackley knew that the bodies had been taken to the potters' field behind the old county poor farm and buried together in an unmarked grave, wrapped only in a canvas tarp. For both Hickey and Josie, the end of life was as unceremonious as the beginning, and no one lamented except the little junkman left crying on the sidewalk.

The Monday after the fire Albert had stoically resumed his daily rounds about town and had resumed his old practice of taking meals at the Soldiers of the Cross. Mr. Benton and the firemen together repaired his damaged roof. Then late one afternoon in early December, just before winter set in, there was a knock on his door. He opened it to Captain Pearce and a stranger.

"Cap'n Pearce," Albert said. "Nice for you to visit me."

"Albert, this is Attorney Hekkema. He has some news for you."

The three men sat at Albert's table and Attorney Hekkema carefully explained that Mr. Bishop had written a book that had made him a lot of money and that he had left a will and a trust to care for Albert with a generous monthly allotment for the rest of his life. Albert was stunned, and tears rolled down his cheek from his one good eye. "Edward, Mr. Bishop, was a prince of a man, a prince of a man."

Captain Pearce and Attorney Hekkema excused themselves and went next door to visit Mr. Benton.

When he finally became aware of the extent of his windfall, Albert, as any typically frugal Dutchman and with Captain Pearce's help, opened a bank account and deposited most of his monthly benefit into savings, holding out just enough to live on and, of course, tithe to the church. Thus, ailing from arthritis and old age, he finally retired from the junk business and parked his pushcart permanently in the old shed next to Hickey's stack of boxes.

CHAPTER TWENTY-NINE

Mysterious Ways

And now that the evil neighbors were dead and the aging Albert was making a significant contribution to the Ambrosia Avenue Church, the dominie and the elders agreed to allow him to become a communicant member, a gesture that comforted Albert after the death of his dearest friends and restored his faith in the basic goodness of the human race.

But the dominie was curious. "How could a little rag picker like Albert Bosch become suddenly affluent enough to give as he does to the church?" he pondered one Sunday noon while I was at their house for dinner. "I know he didn't get rich buying junk from the people and selling it to the Rag & Metal. He must have come into some money somehow. If he has, he may need help managing it. I think I should visit him soon."

And that is how it came to pass that the dominie sat at Albert's table one day in the early spring, drinking coffee with him and discussing matters "of mutual interest."

"Are you getting along on your own, Mr. Bosch?" he asked.

"Oh yes, dominie, I get along just fine. I'm retired now you know. I'm not in the junk business no more."

"Are you independent, or are you collecting a dole from the government?" he asked boldly. "Being your dominie, I bear some responsibility for your well being, you know, and I just want to have the assurance that you are not indigent and if you need any help managing your resources...."

"My friend, my brother, Edward, ...er Mr. Bishop, he made me a bene... bene... finch...."

"Beneficiary?"

"Yes benefinchery."

"Beneficiary to what? Did that old drunkard have life insurance?"

"I don't know if Mr. Bishop had life issurance or not. He gave me some money from his book and Cap'n Pearce from Sodjers of the Cross helps me take care of it. He's a good man.

"Mr. Bishop was a perfesser once you know, a perfesser at the semintary, and he wrote a book, I'll show you," he said, rising from his chair, hobbling to the counter, removing from the drawer his leather bound copy of *Manna* and handing it to him.

The dominie looked at the book, grew pale and numb, began to shake, and laying his head on the table, nearly passed out.

When he was finally able to raise his head, Albert had left the room and returned. "I saved this after the fire," he said, affectionately holding up for the dominie to see, the charred and twisted remains of a once elegant bronze nameplate. You could still read the inscription, *Pieter E. Bisschop, Doctor of Theology*.

"God's ways sure are mysterous," Albert opined. "Like the song we sung Sunday. Mr. Bishop leave me a nice heritance, and Cass leave the boys them ball yards and the Colored boys got a team and the Sodjers of the Cross got a nice new house and a big new dining room and Mr. Benton got a job working for Cap'n Pearce. I don't understand it at all. Mysterous. But I know God done it, domie, I just know God done it."

Dominie VandeBruin was stunned and speechless. After an awkward moment he told Albert he had business to tend to, got up and left, thoughtlessly leaving his hat on Albert's dining table.

CHAPTER THIRTY

The Wisdom of Solomon

With the help of Mr. Benton, Albert sold his collection of relics, including Mama's sewing machine, to an antique dealer for an astonishing sum. After the war the dairy and the police quit using horses, so the fence and the barn came down, and Mr. Benton went to work for Soldiers of the Cross, also with a monthly allotment from Hickey Bishop with the provision that he continue to look after Albert. So life continued on Amity Street for another thirteen years.

Then one Monday morning in May, Albert Bosch died. Mr. Benton found him. It was his habit to check in on Albert regularly, and when he went in that morning he found Albert slumped over his kitchen table. He ran over and told Mrs. Baker and within minutes all of the Dutch of Hackley had received the news of his demise. Stocky, broad-hipped matrons bending over at the waist to pick clothing from their wicker laundry baskets straightened up and called to their neighbors in guttural Dutch brogue, "Albert is dead! Albert Bosch is dead. Mr. Benton found him."

I happened to have taken the day off and had stopped by my mother's for coffee that morning. We were in the back yard, and I was helping her hang the bed sheets on the clothesline. Out of respect and curiosity I walked over to Albert's house. The undertaker had not yet arrived. Mr. Benton, dressed in his khaki Soldiers of the Cross uniform, made no effort to keep me out, so I entered Albert Bosch's house for the first time in my life.

Albert was sitting at his table, head down, his deformed left arm crooked on the table, cradling his head, much the way we used to sit at our desks when our teacher told us to put our heads down. The house was clean and orderly, with dishes stacked neatly on a shelf above the sink. A tin drinking cup stood next to the pump.

"There's boxes in the shed what belong to you," Mr. Benton told me. "Mr. Bishop had Albert store the boxes in there for you, and asked me to be sure you got them, but not until after them and Albert had all died."

I walked around back and opened the door to the shed. There, next to the old pushcart, stacked neatly on a board were five beer cartons, numbered and taped carefully shut, all bearing the inscription, "Save for Christian Weaver." I don't think Hickey ever knew my real name.

The only other thing in the shed was Albert's old pushcart, and for a moment I thought I could hear the ghostly grate of its steel wheel rims on the pavement. As I grasped the dusty handle, I remembered the devilment I had done to poor Albert back in my childhood, and I swelled with a strange mixture of guilt for myself and admiration for the little man I had abused.

Tucked into one of the studs next to his pushcart was a piece of cardboard, the back of a writing pad. I removed it from its niche and turned it over and read the childish scrawl: *wiskie for edwerd*. I laid the cardboard on the top of the stack of boxes.

I went back into the house. Over the table hung a solitary picture: an old silver haired man, hands folded, offering thanks for his bowl of soup and half loaf of bread. Beside Albert on the table was a Bible, pressed open to Proverbs 31 by a large magnifying glass.

"I tried to get him to move," Mr. Benton said, "but he wouldn't. Then I touched him and he was cold and stiff. Must have died yesterday."

We talked for a short time about the old days in the neighborhood and how the block was changing now that many of the Dutch were dying or moving out. Then the undertaker and his assistant arrived and asked us to leave. A short time later they called us back in. Albert's body lay on a stretcher in the middle of the kitchen, his hands neatly folded over his chest, and we four carefully carried him out and placed him into the hearse. They gently closed the door of the big black Cadillac, and drove off.

"Long as you're here, let's load up them boxes and bring them to your house," Mr. Benton offered. "Hang on, just a minute." He went into Albert's house and dialed the telephone. "Honey, can you come over here to Albert's house with the truck. We got some boxes we need to take to Chris Newmyer's house."

A few minutes later a brown pickup truck with the Soldiers of the Cross logo on the door drove into Albert's driveway. A lovely lady about my age opened the door and got out. She was wearing the khaki uniform with captain's bars on the collar. "Remember Audrey?" he asked. "My daughter? Captain Pearce got her a scholarship and she went to college and seminary, and now she is the director of Soldiers of the Cross. The Captain retired two years ago."

I shook Audrey's hand and blinked when I realized I was staring at her, the picture of her sunbathing on the roof of her porch many years ago leaping suddenly into the forefront of the many other pictures crowding my memory that morning.

"The Lord's been real good to us," Mr. Benton continued. "I should retire, but Audrey won't let me, so I'm just working for her a few hours a week. She says it keeps me out of mischief and gives me something to do since mom died." Funny, I'd never seen Mrs. Benton. I never knew she existed.

We loaded the boxes on the back of the pickup truck and they followed me to my mother's house.

The Wisdom of Solomon

Before they left he helped me carry the boxes into the basement.

"You should stay now for supper," my mother offered, "I still got some roast left from yesterday. I can't eat a whole roast by myself you know."

"Thanks, Mom, but I've got to be getting along. I still got a deadline to meet by tomorrow and I need time to write my new piece. I want to get back for Albert's funeral though, so be sure to call me and let me know when it is."

She kissed me goodbye and I drove away.

CHAPTER THIRTY-ONE

A Stately Event

Albert's funeral was a stately event. Colorful flowers on wicker stands flanked his bronze casket, which was draped with a spray of yellow chrysanthemums and the words *Friend and Neighbor* emblazoned in gold letters on a red silken banner. The firemen from Number Two Station had canvassed the neighborhoods for donations to cover funeral costs, and everyone contributed generously.

Mrs. Boot, the church soloist sang "In the Sweet Bye and Bye," and "Does Jesus Care?" Then the organist played other grand old hymns of the church while six uniformed firemen marched up the aisle at attention and sat in the front row. Mr. Benton and Audrey sat in the front row dressed in their uniforms, Dutch ladies, clad in black dresses, black gloves and black hats lifted their veils and daubed their eyes with tatted white hankies, while the Dutch men, unused to being shaved and dressed in their Sunday suits on Thursday, sat stroking their chins as the Reverend John Vande-Bruin delivered a message sprinkled liberally with scriptures welcoming the good and faithful servant into the kingdom prepared for him by his heavenly Father. He praised Albert's simple, unwavering faith, his devotion to duty and his unconditional love for others. Mainly he thanked Albert for the lessons he taught the rest of us about humility, perseverance, brotherhood and long suffering. And he spoke of God's mysterious ways. His tone was gentler and his words more kindly than any I'd ever heard him utter before.

I sat in the back row where Albert used to sit and watched as the rows of mourners were ushered past the chancel for their last look at the little old junkman. Calvin came and sat next to me. We were among the last to pass by the casket, and the transformation I saw stunned me. Albert's matted, stringy hair had been washed and neatly combed. The anguish in his face had dissolved into peace, the squint of his eye and the painful wrinkles of his cheeks had vanished under the soothing hand of the undertaker. The tightly drawn corner of his mouth had melted into a contented smile.

He was dressed, neither in the typical overalls and blue work shirt he usually wore, nor the old suit Josie had tailored for him, but rather in a new, neatly tailored charcoal suit, white shirt and striped tie. In his good arm he cradled a leather bound copy of *Manna*.

The firemen carried the casket from the church and placed it in the hearse, which followed the fire chief's red Ford down Ambrosia Avenue, siren wailing at every corner. At the cemetery, Reverend Vande-Bruin said the ashes to ashes words while the firemen lowered the casket and every man threw a handful of dirt into the grave. When the procession left, men in work clothes appeared to finish filling the grave and cover it with the squares of sod that stood next to the pile of dirt.

After the funeral Calvin and I went out to dinner together and caught each other up on the missing years. He and his sister Grace had both become schoolteachers, but not in Hackley. We promised to stay in touch.

On Saturday the firemen came and burned Albert's house down. They did it carefully and slowly, the flames never getting out of control. Thick clouds of acrid smoke hung somberly and ceremoniously over the houses, seeming to plunge the neighborhood into mourning. Later in the afternoon, as the last embers of ash began to cool, city workers loaded the final debris into a dump truck and raked the ground level. Then they all left.

Only the memory of Albert Bosch, a scorched circle of earth, and the smell of burned tarpaper lingered on Amity Street.

CHAPTER THIRTY-TWO

Where Tulips Once Bloomed

One warm Saturday evening last summer while returning from a trip, I took a detour and went back to Hackley to visit my mother. My dad had died and I had been trying to talk her into moving into the high rise, without much success. Together we decided to take a drive through town.

The old Number Two Fire Station on Wood Street has been preserved by the city as a museum. One bay contains the old red hook 'n ladder, still as shiny as it was when I was a boy. A friendly old retired fireman who remembers the fatal fires oversees the premises and lets visitors climb up and sit in the driver's seat at the tail end of the ladders and turn the big old wooden steering wheel. The other bay contains the familiar old red pumper truck and the shiny red Ford pickup with the big chrome siren on the fender that the chief used to drive. In a neatly landscaped spot in front of the old firehouse stands Albert Bosch's pushcart, freshly painted a glossy green. When I close my eyes I can still see little Albert pushing his cart down Amity Street, and I can hear the grate of the wheels on the pavement.

Two blocks further down the street is the cemetery in which my father is buried. Just inside the front entrance to the right of the gate is a marble monument topped with a cross and bearing the inscription, *Albert Bosch, Died May 5, 1958*.

Amity Street has fallen into disrepair. It is not the neat Dutch Ghetto any more, but a ghetto of poverty, prejudice and despair. Crabgrass covers the ground where tulips once bloomed, the shrubbery has grown into grotesque shapes, the lawns are bare, and most of the neat old Dutch homes are torn down, burned down, boarded up or painted preposterous colors. Battered cars are parked awkwardly on the streets as though they had been abandoned. Albert's and Hickey's lots are vacant and overgrown with weeds. Baker's and Benton's houses have both burned down. Untouched by any caring hand, my old neighborhood stands a peeling monument to neglect, prejudice and abuse.

The celery fields have vanished, prey to neglect, erosion, greedy streams and briar bushes. The creek has devolved into little rivulets and scummy ponds.

Two bright spots illumine the neighborhood. One is the beautiful, spacious *Albert Bosch Memorial Building* that houses the Soldiers of the Cross. The other, behind it, is the *Casien White Memorial Field*, where, under the supervision of volunteers from the Veterans' Association, happy youngsters of all nations and colors play baseball together. The infield is neatly sculpted and the outfield grass carefully mowed.

I stopped for a few moments to watch a team practice. A Black coach hit a grounder to a white boy playing shortstop. He scooped it up, tossed it to a darker skinned boy playing second who wheeled beautifully and fired it to a Black boy playing first. I guess the old drunks didn't dream in vain after all. They left a legacy that totally baffled those who were blind in spirit.

On the east side of town the decaying old county poor house still looms over a barren landscape, windows broken and crumbling brick walls covered with graffiti. Out back is an overgrown meadow that was once the cemetery for the indigent. Remnants of a rotted wooden fence surround the final resting place of the unblessed. Anonymous caring hands once erected little piles of stones to mark the graves. Those rude monuments are mortared together by time and remain undisturbed, even by the vandals who have defaced the building. Broken pieces of old fruit jars are scattered about, silent testimony that in a time gone by someone knew and cared enough to bring flowers.

If there ever was a record of where Cass, Hickey and Josie lie, it has been has been discarded with other useless bits of history.

CHAPTER THIRTY-THREE

The Gun

"You've got to move, mother," I insisted. "It isn't safe here for you anymore and I can't come home to maintain the place. You've got to sell."

For the first time, she didn't disagree with me. "Yes," she said, "I suppose it's time. I have a lot of friends in the high rise and they all go out together and take bus trips. I've come to grips with it. It's time to go. But first you have to take care of those boxes in the basement. I can't take those into an apartment."

That evening I began to go through Hickey's papers. I was amazed at the lucidity and the precision with which he kept a record of his life. What I discovered in those boxes was the history of a most amazing man. Until that night, I thought he was no more than an eloquent, sometimes angry, gluttonous, misunderstood drunk with a soft heart.

I pored through the papers late into the night, totally absorbed by the memories and the unveiling of the broken professor. It was nearly midnight when my mother came to the foot of the stairs. "Why don't you put that old stuff away for the night, stay over and go to church with me tomorrow?" she asked. Tired after sorting through just three of the five boxes, I agreed and went upstairs to spend the night in my old room. In the morning I awakened to the seductive smell of beef being seared in the roaster.

We ate breakfast together and went to the Ambrosia Avenue Church where I had another surprise. After singing several songs of praise accompanied by a guitar, drums and a keyboard, Pastor John delivered a powerful and sincere message from Matthew about sheep and goats, about Christ coming to judge the living and the dead, and about it being our job just to love without prejudice. He confessed that he was as guilty as any of us for trying to usurp the throne of God and judge others, and that he's had to repent a multitude of times for failing to love others as the Lord has loved us. He declared that we have a profound duty to reach out to others, to love the unlovable and to touch the untouchable just as Jesus reached out and touched the lepers and prostitutes in his day.

After the service he not only shook my hand but also put his arm around me, and with a tear in his eye said, "It's so good to see you again, Chris. One of these weekends when Cal comes home it would be nice if you could come for Sunday dinner, like in the old days." I responded that I would like that, and said that I would get in touch with Calvin and arrange for both of us to be home at the same time.

During dinner mother and I talked about a lot of things. We remembered how dad used to save a piece of roast beef to eat with his pudding and how we used to sit around the table as a family, recite our memory verses and answer questions about the sermon. But I didn't tell her what I had read in Hickey's note pads. Then I returned to the basement to finish sorting through the last two boxes.

The fourth box contained another stack of yellow note pads, the most stunning yet. They told the entire story from the fire at Cass's house to the last days that Hickey and Josie spent together in the small house on Amity Street. Surprisingly they were mostly happy days, days of quiet resolve and contentment punctuated by bouts of drunkenness when Hickey just could not resist the need to escape into the stupor that the whiskey offered.

In the fifth box was a stack of bulletins from the Ambrosia Avenue Church and a collection of old editions of *The Clarion* that contained quotes from *Manna* and articles about the seminary and its graduates, including Reverend John VandeBruin.

And there were two large manila envelopes. The first envelope contained the twisted remains of the bronze nameplate, carefully wrapped in tissue paper, with the inscription, *Pieter E. Bisschop, Doctor of Theology*.

But what I found next stunned me most. I opened the second envelope and was shocked to find a twenty-

The Gun

two caliber pistol wrapped in an old Memphis Red Sox baseball cap, and a note in Hickey's shaky handwriting, "This is the gun that killed Casien White."

The afternoon had passed quickly. Mother had taken a long nap after our Sunday noon dinner. Tradition was that before evening services we would eat a bologna sandwich with potato chips and coffee. As we ate, I talked with her about some of the things I read in Hickey's notes. She was fascinated. "Sounds to me like you've got the makings of a book there," she suggested. We skipped church that evening and spent the time together reminiscing about the old days in the neighborhood, of Albert and his wagon, of youth league baseball, of school, church and catechism, and of Sunday noon dinners. After a last cup of coffee and the traditional cookie, we went to bed. The next morning I packed the boxes into my car and took the envelope to the police station.

When I entered the police station, the overweight, balding sergeant sitting at a desk....

The End

Legion ...
A Man Possessed

A Short Story by Robert Sikkenga

OG

"If it isn't one Eusebius it's another," I grinned as I glanced at the man framed in the doorway of my little room. "Your friend from Nicomedia left just a few minutes ago after foolishly trying to persuade me that Arius of Alexandria has any understanding whatsoever of the deity. Come in."

He opened his arms in a gesture of friendship as we stood in the doorway of my little upstairs room overlooking the city of Nicea and the lovely lake beyond. "Good to see you again Og," he said as he hugged me warmly, his arms just fitting around my waist and the top of his bald head barely reaching the tip of my beard. "It's good to see you again. How was your trip from Bashan?"

"It had its ups and downs, literally as well as figuratively. The aspect of the journey that blessed me most was that we followed the path Paul took on his second journey. As we went through such cities as Antioch, Derbe, Lystra and Iconium I felt that we were walking on hallowed ground. Even after three hundred years his spirit still haunts those places. That man was truly amazing! But Nicea is a long way from Kursi, and as you know it's nothing but mountains all the way through Cappadocia. It was a long, hard trip. Very tiring. The best thing was that the thieves left us alone. I guess they thought we were too poor to bother with. But I doubt if I'd made the journey had the emperor's summons sounded less urgent. How was your trip from Caesarea?"

"We avoided the perils of the mountains, but chose instead the perils of the sea. It was longer but less grueling. We encountered two storms along the way and I lost some of my papers in the first one. We sailed all the way from Caesarea to a fishing village opposite Chalcedon. From there it was a short jaunt. You may want to consider going back that way with us when this business is finished."

"I may never go back at all," I said mischievously, "this is a beautiful land. Up here in the north the air is very pleasant. That lake is as calm as I've ever seen any lake. And it doesn't appear to rile up like the Tiberius. Can you believe that I grew up on the sea and can't tolerate it? The very thought of sailing makes me seasick."

"I don't much blame you, this is a spellbinding sight right here out your window, Og, especially at sunset," he said as he pushed back my curtain. "My window faces the opposite direction."

He called me Og in a playful sort of way because in ancient days my land was called Bashan and it had a king named Og who was about as big as I am. Moses massacred Og and his entire army at Endrei even before the Israelites crossed the Jordan.

"I've had a long time to think about the issue facing us at this council, my conciliatory friend," I said, "and after such an arduous trip, I'm in no mood to compromise with anyone who questions the eternal divinity of Christ. As far as I'm concerned, Arius of Alexandria and his gang work at Satan's bidding when they portray him as nothing more than a mere mortal."

"Don't be so hard on him," the Bishop of Caesarea urged, "he's deeply committed to the concept of monotheism and is afraid that the notion of a pluralistic godhead will only propel us back to the days of the pagans. Heaven will become Olympus all over again."

"I almost wish that Licinius had prevailed over Constantine," I said.

"At least when the he was persecuting the church we were not divided. Now, with our first taste of freedom under an emperor who calls himself a Christian, we begin to quarrel. As in the old days, it seems we blossom under persecution and become fragmented in times of ease."

"That's where I believe you and I see eye to eye," he said, restoring to his face his diplomatic smile. "We must remain unified. And when there is disagreement among us, we must search for a common ground. I'm sure we can phrase things in a manner that satisfies both sides."

"Unity at the expense of truth?" I asked. "Never. I'm in a far better position to understand the nature of Jesus than that mindless Egyptian. If he's not careful he'll bring down those horrible plagues on his house again. Wouldn't it be a good joke if those little green frogs began to jump out of his bed and his breadbasket?"

"Be thoughtful and compassionate, my friend," he pleaded. "This is a serious controversy. What we declare here in Nicea may well decide the way the church understands the nature of Christ for all time. All of the bishops have gathered here to work it through and to frame a statement that reflects our common thought. It is important that we leave here undivided."

"I understand the value of unity, my brother," I answered, raising my voice, "but I will not compromise the truth to attain it. On that point I will not be moved. I think Arius and his cohorts are a loud but distinct minority. On our way through the mountains we were joined by brothers from Cappadocia, and all agree that the Father and the Son are of one substance, distinct but equally divine. That's not polytheistic because, as the Master himself said, 'I and the father are one'."

As if by manipulation, his joviality returned. "Are you going to bring old Legion's story to the dais?" he asked.

"Better than that," I asserted, reaching for the document. "I've composed a narrative, in the first person, recounting the story as it has been handed down through the generations. I've spent years assigning my young scribes to copy it. I'm going to read it aloud, and when I'm finished I'll give each of the brothers a copy. I have enough for all. If, as you call him, 'Legion's' own testimony is not convincing, I'm afraid the church of Jesus Christ is marching headlong into darkness."

He took a copy of my story, and with a smile, promised to read it that very night.

In the Chamber

When it finally became my turn to address the bishops gathered in the great hall of the imperial palace at Nicea, I approached the dais and gazed intently at the hundreds seated by rank on the benches that ran down both sides of the hall.

What one saw from the dais could both break the heart and engender unfettered joy. They sat quietly at first, men from all over the world, each wearing the garb and bearing the cultural distinctions of his native country. The church of Jesus Christ was certainly not a provincial body, but a cloud of witnesses of all colors and of varying thoughts, histories and habits. Though someday in paradise all would be wearing white robes and singing the same song, on this devil-filled earth arriving at a consensus was sure to be a most daunting task.

There was one sign of unity: in every corner of the room men from Hispania to Egypt and Gaul to Armenia bore the scars of the same persecution: missing limbs, gouged out eyes and burned flesh witnessed silently to the unifying and emboldening power of the Holy Spirit.

As I began my talk, I prayed that such a spirit would prevail here today.

"Thank you, my brothers, fellow princes of the church. We are gathered here in this great hall at the bidding of our emperor to resolve a matter that has caused riots and threatens to divide the church forever: the nature of Jesus Christ. Please, before you arrive at any conclusions, hear the testimony of a bygone saint who stood in the very presence of God and experienced his singular deity in a mighty way."

The followers of Arius began to taunt me, but when the emperor turned toward them they turned suddenly silent. I began to read....

Legion

"I've always loved the hills and the wind and the water. As a youngster I used to slide down the rocky hillside below Gergesa and stand on the plateau looking out over the deep blue Sea of Tiberius. I enjoyed watching the fishermen as they flung their nets and dragged in their catch of fish. I don't know why, but one small blue boat that often sailed from the direction of Capernaum caught my fancy. Its fishermen seemed different in some unexplainable way.

"I was a very private lad and spent much time alone. As I roamed the meadows, I pondered and I sang. Sometimes I turned and faced the hills, and shouted whatever poetic fancy entered my head and poured out through my lips. The hills would answer back, sometimes repeating what I had told them, and sometimes garbling my words into utterances of tongues unknown. I never knew what the hills would say to me, and I was enchanted by the voices that spoke in what I thought to be eloquent tones.

"I liked watching the wind as much as speaking with it. The cool breeze bearing its clouds of dust would spiral around the mountain peaks behind me, gather speed and race downward, blowing the little boats out toward the middle of the sea. Sometimes it would swirl around me, wrapping my hair around my neck and trying to tear the cloak off my body. Sometimes I had to hang on to a bush or an outcropping of rock to keep my balance.

"I knew the storm was coming before the sailors did. The fishermen, intent on their nets, seemed not to notice the birds diving for cover up in the hills as the wind circled and mustered for an attack on the warm water far below. Suddenly, as if on command from some higher power, the winds would charge the sea and instantly stir up tumultuous waves, sometimes capsizing the little boats before the fishermen even knew they were in trouble. Then the air became calm but the sea continued to boil as though the winds themselves had dived into the abyss and were churning its depths, waiting for a command to surge upward again to challenge those who dared invade the sanctity of the deep.

"Fishermen clung to their capsized boats and waited to be rescued. Sometimes the boats broke apart, and the sailors held fast to the floating masts. I watched anxiously as they let the surging waves carry them to shore. Once I watched as one sailor perished no more than a bowshot from the beach.

"I fancied myself an ascetic, a stranger from humanity, at one with nature, in harmony with the forces that no one else could feel or understand. The wind took on personality, and each new breeze was a new spirit, an innocent friendly ghost only I knew. In my imagination I romped with my sprightly friends, and we danced and reveled and talked together.

"The plateau overlooking the sea was our playground. We pranced through the fields where farmers raised grain and lambs on the flat projection that jutted from the mountains above. Priests from the temple of Zeus kept their sacred swine on the side closest to the cliffs, where they rooted for scraps thrown there by reapers and the men who slaughtered the sheep. The priests kept them from wandering too close to the precipice that plunged to the sea more than a thousand cubits below. To the east, where the level plateau suddenly met the mountain, were the tombs, carved into the face of the jagged cliff.

"In retrospect, in my old age, I give the winds and the waves character, not simply as a poetic figure of speech, but because in truth, they did have character. They were alive with spirits, evil spirits from the demon gods, a fact of which I did not become aware until I was grown. Had I known that, I would never have made the phantoms of the breeze my friends.

"One day shortly after I had barely turned twenty, a particularly gentle zephyr floated down the mountainside, rippled the grass as it passed through the field on the plateau, and seemed to swirl in place as it ruffled my hair and caressed my face. The wind gave me a name. 'Son of Hermes,' it said playfully, 'walk with me across the plateau and down to the tombs.' Enchanted, I followed.

"At the tombs other voices began to speak to me. 'You are a handsome lad,' one said, 'well suited to be the messenger of the gods.'

"Another added, 'You please Diana. She would be delighted to have you as her lover.' I was seduced by their flattery.

"Then their discourse took a different turn. 'Son of Hades,' one of them said, 'pick up this sharp stone and scrape it on your arm. Feel the pain.' Unable to resist, I did as commanded. 'Did you ever think there could be so much pleasure in pain?' the voice said with a sneering laugh. Terrified, I ran from the tombs, screaming, stumbling over the stones that lined the space between the tombs and the grain fields, and flew home as fast as I could.

"Our house was on the southwestern edge of the great city of Gergesa. From my window I could look down and see the marketplace, the temples of Zeus and Artemis, and the theater. To the east of the marketplace stood the stadium where sometimes the Jewish boys from the other side of the sea would wander over to watch our naked athletes run their races and play other games.

"I couldn't tell my mother what had happened. She'd think I was possessed. So I just sat by the tree, in the shelter of the mountain that protected my home from the ferocious winds that sometimes ripped their way through the hills and woods around Gergesa.

"After I first cut myself with the sharp stone, it was three days before I dared wander back to the plateau where I'd heard the voices. Then I slid down the path gingerly, looking constantly to my left and right, and I sat in the shadow of a great rock, waiting.

"Soon it came. The same gentle breeze that had wrapped its arms around me a few days before. 'Where have you been, son of Hermes. We've missed you,' it said with a congenial laugh. I felt it enfold me again, and I tried to wriggle loose, but it said, 'I'm not letting you go. I'm going to stay with you, stay closer to you than your own skin. We have a mission for you. Let's go to the priest.'

"We walked to the temple of Zeus, still there in its splendor from the days of the Greeks, but now in the keeping of Roman priests. 'Ask the priest about the Jewish Messiah,' the voice, now inside me, said.

"I wandered around the columns, stunned by the magnificence of the place, but feeling foreign because I was by birth a Geshurite, my ancestors being refugees who fled from Canaan before Joshua's onslaught. Even after all those years, we still felt that we belonged to Baal, though we had no altars, no temples and no priests. But traditions are slow to die.

"Finally a priest appeared. 'Ask him about the Jewish Messiah,' the voice within me said.

"'Sir,' I asked, 'can you tell me about the Jewish Messiah?'

'He looked at me strangely. 'How do you know about that?' he asked, looking about as though uncomfortable and impatient.

"'I don't know. I must have heard somebody talking about it,' I stammered, groping for an answer.

"'Those Jews have strange ideas,' he said, for some reason now suddenly willing to take the time to talk to me. 'They think they are going to be redeemed, set free from Roman control. They seem to think a hero will rise from among them with supernatural powers and will raise an army that will drive out the Romans, much like the Maccabees drove out the Greeks. But the joke will be on them. When they rebel, we'll destroy Jerusalem and burn their temple. The emperor said so.'

"'Ask him about Jesus,' the voice said.

"'Sir,' I said, 'can you tell me about Jesus?'

"He looked at me with a frown. 'Who told you about him?'

"'I don't know. I just heard people talking.'

"'He's just another one of a bunch of itinerant preachers over on the other side. He wanders from Magdala up to Capernaum, Bethsaida and Korazin. They say he's quite entertaining, doing a lot of magic, healing people, and,' he added with a sneering laugh, 'even raising the dead.'

"'And the Jews think he is going to start a rebellion?'

"'They do. At least some of them do. He gathers a crowd, and his followers grow in number every day. His worst enemies are his own people, though. He constantly harangues the priests and the Pharisees and the Sadducees. He doesn't seem to be as much in rebellion against Rome as he is against his own authorities. But we're keeping an eye on him.'

"With that I returned home. I climbed the hill and sat under the tree, protected from the wind. Then the voice spoke. 'This Jesus is not an enemy of Rome,' it said, 'he is our enemy, the enemy of the gods. There has been a spiritual war going on since the dawn of time, and a major battle is about to begin. This Jesus is going to attack us. He's not an ordinary man or even a powerful prophet. He's the commander of the army of Jehovah, come to make war on us. He attacked Bacchus, the god of wine, over in Cana, and he is planning to attack Demeter, the goddess of the harvest, on that hillside near Bethsaida. He boldly calls himself "the Bread of Life." He intends to start his church right here in our country. His purpose in coming here isn't to redeem the Jews from the Romans. He's come to try to take back his creation, to win the people back from us.'

"'From us,' I asked, 'who are we?'

"'My young friend, we are members of Satan's army. We once lived in heaven as angels, but we were not content to be servants to Jehovah. So we rebelled. We tried to usurp God's throne, but his army of angels defeated us and drove us out. Ever since then we have been fighting as exiled rebels, tempting the woman in Eden, inspiring the men of Babel to invade the heavens, giving the people gods and idols and temples and worship rituals that appeal to their carnal nature. Now we hover everywhere, encouraging greed and lust.

'Now God himself has taken on human form by being born of a woman and coming to this earth to make war on us. We've challenged him everywhere. In an effort to kill him as a baby, we induced Herod to murder all the children in the Bethlehem region. Over on the other side of the sea, we incited the men of Nazareth to drive him to the cliff at the edge of town and throw him over. But he cast a spell on them and walked right through the crowd. So far we've lost every battle, but we won't quit. Now we've got a new plan and intend to execute it at this very place on which we stand.

'This is our place. We live in the mountains behind you. We ride on the wind. We live in the depths of the seas with Poseidon and under the earth with Hades. We created all of those pagan gods. We even created the Baal that your ancestors worshipped. I called you a son of Hermes because he is the messenger of those gods and you are to be our messenger. We will put the words in you, and you will say them. Come down to the plateau tomorrow and I will introduce you to more of us.'

"I felt trapped. I no longer belonged to myself. I felt exposed. I had no private thoughts anymore. The voice was there all the time. Even when it wasn't talking to me, I could sense its presence, owning me, controlling me. Early the next morning, under compulsion, I went back to the plateau.

"'Look down there to the sea,' the voice within said. 'Do you see that fishing boat? The blue one heading southward from Capernaum? Jesus is on that boat with his disciples. Keep your eye out for that boat. Someday it will come here. When it does, there will be conflict, and you will be in the center of it. Our plan is to lure him here to the plateau where he will confront you and try to drive us out of you. We will raise a violent response, charge him, cause the swine to stampede, and hopefully drive him over the cliff to his doom. Now come with me to the tombs.'

"At the tombs more voices began to speak out, quietly at first, then growing in intensity until they were screaming. It was such a cacophony of noise that I couldn't distinguish one voice from another. Finally one screamed louder than the rest, 'Pick up a sharp rock! Cut yourself! It will give you great joy!'

"Unable to restrain myself, I picked up a sharp stone and scraped my arm until I drew blood. It hurt, but it felt better than before. 'Cut your legs!' the voice shouted, so I reached down and gouged the skin from my ankles and my shins. It hurt, but I had to continue. The scraping made the pain go away but at the same time brought more pain in its place. And the pain was good. I held the stone in my hand and turned toward home, screaming in joyous misery.

"My mother met me at the foot of the lane. 'What happened to you?' she shouted, with terror in her voice. 'You're bleeding! Did the robbers attack you?'

"When I opened my mouth to answer, words came out, but they weren't my words. The voice was mine, but the words belonged to the demon inside me. 'I'm a messenger of the gods,' I screamed, 'and we are at war with the devil.' I knew it was a lie. I knew the demons were at war with the one true God, but I had no control over my tongue. Satan was lying through me. Driven, I began to limp around in circles, kicking at rocks and hitting trees with my fists, skinning my knuckles until they bled.

"My mother put her hands over her face and cried. The neighbors heard me and came running over. They tried to restrain me. When they put their hands on me, I felt a strength surge through me that I had never felt before. With a sweeping motion of both my arms I threw the men from me and ran back to the plateau, taking refuge in the shadows of the tombs. There was no hospitable place for me on the face of the earth.

"As night began to fall, I heard them coming after me, chains clanking on the stones that lined the path. Without knowing why, I sat docilely by while six men wrapped me in chains and tied the chains to a large rock at the entrance to a cave. No one spoke until I was fastened securely to the rock. 'I think that will keep him,' the heavy one said.

"'What the rats from the tombs don't eat tonight, the birds will in the morning,' a bald headed stranger added.

"'I always knew this boy would end up this way,' declared the man who dragged the chains down the path. 'He always was a dreamer and a fool. Opened himself right up to the demons. Must be a thousand of them in him the way he was ranting. Now they can get into the rats and the birds.'

"As they backed away, content that I was securely fastened to the rock, I stood up and screamed. They turned and looked at me without compassion, contempt etched into their faces. I flexed my muscles with all my might and burst the chains that wrapped me. Stunned and afraid, they ran toward the city, and I ran to the far end of the tombs. Then I collapsed.

"When I awoke, the sun was shining brightly, and my arms and legs and chest ached from the stress of breaking the chains. My cloak was torn and spattered with blood. I ripped it from me, threw it away, and stood stark naked among the dead in the tombs. Then I walked slowly toward the plateau. When I came near where the herd of swine was rooting among the rubbish, I sat down among them and began to eat the meat left on the bone by the men who butchered the sheep. It was still warm and fresh. It tasted good.

"When I was full, I walked back to the field of grain and lay down to rest. The warm sun soothed my aching back. I don't know how long I slept.

"For the next several days I wandered from the fields to the tombs. I spent my days roaming back and forth between the hills and the edge of the city, hoping to catch a glimpse of my mother. Whenever I neared the gates of Gergesa, people ran shouted warnings of my approach. I never tried to hurt anyone. I just turned and went back to the plateau.

"I sunned myself in the grain fields and sat in the shade of the olive trees higher in the hills. I ate with the swine, and at night slept near the tombs. The demons owned me, but for now they were silent. Sometimes I could feel them writhing within me, as though preparing for the battle to come.

"One day, for a reason beyond my understanding, I wandered to the edge of the plateau where the swine were feeding and began to watch a fishing boat sail from Capernaum toward Gergesa. As it neared I could see the fishermen on board, casting their nets and hauling in their catch of fish. It was the blue boat from Capernaum.

"I sensed the winds swirling nervously among the crags high above me, impatient to rush down and attack the blue boat, but waiting for the right moment. Then suddenly, as the boat neared the shoals below me, the wind exploded into a thousand tempests, stormed down the face of the mountain, bounced off the crags and struck the water at the bow of the little blue boat. The fishermen, caught in the middle of hauling in their nets, abandoned them and stumbled around on the deck, franticly reaching for a rail or a rope to cling to. Then the most amazing thing happened.

"I knew it was Jesus. I don't know how I knew, I just knew. With the wind tearing at his cloak, he stepped calmly from the cabin below out onto the pitching deck, looked to the sky and raised his hands. And when he did, the wind suddenly stopped blowing, the waves flattened out, and the sea was calmer than I had ever seen it before. The fishermen stood, astonished, and knelt at his feet as if in worship. The demons within me shuddered.

"Some of the sailors began to gesture, as if to beg him to turn around and head back to the Jewish side of the sea, but he was determined to come ashore at Gergesa. Taking up their oars, they rowed around the rocks to the land. I wanted to warn them that they were being lured into a trap, but the spirits within me smothered that wish and ignited an angry fury in my soul.

"They towed their boat up to beach, and I went forward to meet them. For a moment I felt hospitable toward them, but as they approached the demons turned my conviviality to antagonism. Feelings of aggression welled up within me, and when Jesus stepped up, looked me in the eye and asked my name, I took a deep breath, opened my mouth and my lungs erupted with a torrent of abuse.

"The demon within me screamed, 'My name is Legion; for we are many!' thinking perhaps to intimidate him either by virtue of their numbers or by identifying with the legion of Roman soldiers stationed in the garrison nearby.

"But the fierce tirade didn't seem to bother him. In a tone of absolute authority, he simply ordered the demons to leave me. Suddenly the angry churning within me turned to fear. I felt the spirits tremble, then their fear turned to panic. They had been defeated by just a word from the Creator of heaven and earth, and they were terrified, not knowing what he would do with them.

"'What have you to do with me, Jesus, Son of the Most High God? I beseech you, do not torment me,' the demon pleaded, using my tongue. 'Don't send us into the abyss where we will be scorned and reviled,' another screamed in sudden cowardice, 'send us anywhere, even into the swine! Please!'

"With a victorious smile he obliged. The demons poured out of me, and in a moment the herd of swine began to snort and buck and run in circles. The swineherds trembled and froze in fear as the normally docile beasts became enraged, and suddenly, as if by command, bolted toward the precipice and one by one tumbled over the edge and plunged into the rocky abyss below, carrying the demons with them. The herdsmen fled to the city.

"The same calm that came over the sea came over me. One of the fishermen ran to the boat and brought me a cloak, which I wrapped about myself. I prostrated myself at his feet, and knew that this Jewish Messiah was none other than God almighty clothed in human flesh. I wanted nothing more than to be with him, to get into his boat and escape forever from that cruel land.

"People from town slowly began to arrive, having been told by the swineherds what had happened. They were afraid, but curious. The herdsmen explained how Jesus ordered the demons out of me and into the swine. The people were amazed, but frightened. I stood up and told them not to fear, that Jesus was a good man, a holy man. But the priests who kept the swine declared otherwise, and told the townspeople not to trust a Jew who would destroy their sacred animals. The people became angry and shaking their fists and waving sticks and rocks, urged him to leave.

"He simply smiled, beckoned to the fishermen, and walked back down toward the boat. My peace slipped slowly away. I followed him and begged, 'Please take me with you. I don't want to stay here anymore. Please, Lord, I want only to be with you. I can't stay here. I'm loathed here. I'm scorned. They will kill me. Let me go with you.'

"I'll never forget his response. 'Return to your home, and declare how much God has done for you.' It was simple. It was direct. It was powerful. It gave me overwhelming peace and a resolute sense of mission. 'Declare how much God has done for you.' I turned and went home, full of anticipation.

"My mother welcomed me. I calmly told her what had happened. She was my first convert to Jesus Christ. No more memories of Baal. No more bowing to the Roman gods.

"The men who had chained me were the most curious. They listened intently as I exuberantly related the story of my redemption from the demons. As they listened their faces brightened, and the truth of the one true God burrowed its way into their hearts. And they went home and told their families.

"As the days passed, more and more people stopped in the streets of Gergesa to listen to my story. An unknown power moved me and seized them. I talked and they believed. And they went home and told their loved ones. And they too believed.

"Then one day the power of the Spirit took me back to the plateau. People followed. And when I looked out to the sea, the little blue boat was nearing the shore. 'He's coming back!' I shouted, 'Jesus is coming back.'

I ran down to meet him, and he and his disciples climbed the path up to the plateau. They greeted me warmly.

"The word spread quickly, and the people flocked from the city to see him. He stood on a promontory and began to speak. The people sat. He talked and they listened. He blessed them and their children. He spoke of love and life abundant. And he told them of the kingdom of heaven.

"They brought their lame, their sick, their dumb, their deaf, their possessed, and he healed them all! They sat all day as he taught about the love of almighty God and the forgiveness of sins. When evening came, they were hungry, but they wouldn't go home.

"Jesus asked his disciples, 'How many people are here?'

"'About four thousand,' they answered.

"'How many loaves of bread do you have?' he asked.

"'Seven' they replied.

"'Give them to me,' he said.

"They gave him the loaves and he began to break them in pieces and give them back to his disciples to distribute to the crowd. It was the most amazing thing I had ever seen. The bread didn't run out. He kept breaking the loaves and giving them out and they multiplied miraculously. When they had finished eating, he asked his disciples to pick up the leftover pieces of bread.

"'How many baskets do you have left over?' he asked.

"'Seven' they replied, as they headed back to the boat. I walked down the hill with them.

"'Do you understand the significance of what happened tonight?' he asked me.

"'No,' I replied.

"'Seven loaves of the bread of life for the seven nations I exiled from the land of Canaan over a thousand years ago. The gospel is for them too. Now, my friend, go feed my sheep.' He and the disciples boarded the little blue boat and rowed toward Capernaum. It was the last time I ever saw him.

"Some of his followers came back and told us that his own people had had him crucified, but that he rose again and ascended to heaven, from whence he came. They explained how his disciples had been filled with the Holy Spirit and had begun to witness boldly for him just as I had done.

"Those followers stayed among us and started a church, right there outside the gates of Zeus's temple. Soon the entire city of Gergesa believed that Jesus the Jewish Messiah was none other than the creator of the universe incarnate, God himself come down to dwell among us, to teach us, to be the sacrifice for our sin, and to make his dwelling in our hearts.

"This my testimony. I'm old now. All of this happened over forty years ago. Since the day of that great battle between God and Satan here on the plateau of Gergesa I have continued to tell all who would listen what God has done for me. Hear my witness, and if anyone ever doubts that Jesus Christ is anything less than almighty God, let him hear my words and believe."

I paused for a long time, allowing the brothers to absorb the words of my ancient countryman. Then I concluded my talk.

"I have two brief points to make while the pages are distributing copies of testimony offered by my witness, known to us only today by a name the demons gave him, 'Legion.'

"My first point is this: there can be no argument about the nature or substance of Jesus Christ. He is the Word that the apostle John confirmed was one with God, the Word made flesh. On the plain below Kursi, formerly known as Gergesa, he manifested omnipotent control over all of the nature that he had created, and absolute power over all of Satan's demons.

Only the God who created all things has the authority to do that.

"My second point is this: we are called to witness, not to adjudicate or dispute among ourselves. God doesn't need judges and lawyers to argue and defend the nature of his being. He wants only witnesses, humble people who simply tell the world what he has done for them. If we are but obedient to that commission, our almighty God will reveal himself to the world through us. This is the primary duty of the church.

"He commissioned my countryman, old 'Legion,' just to testify, to tell what he had seen and what the Lord had done for him, and when he did, God gave increase to the church. Four thousand souls became the first gentile church on the eastern shore of the Sea of Tiberius just because one man told the story of his redemption by the hand of God.

"God can defend himself, my friends, he can guard his own name. He calls his church to be his witnesses in the uttermost parts of the earth, and when we do his bidding, he will give the increase. But if we argue and debate things far beyond our ken, schisms will occur, the body of Christ will be divided, and the church will soon be plunged into darkness.

"The issue that truly confronts us today is not the composition of the godhead, but the mission of the church. When the persecutions of Licinius ended, Satan saw an opportunity to destroy the unity that oppression rendered unto us. He saw an opportunity to end our witnessing, and he used the mind of one of the princes to hinder the mission of the church."

At that remark a mumbling arose among the followers of the Presbyter of Alexandria, and as if on cue they began as one to chant their derisive little ditty about a time when there was no Christ. But the rest of the body cast scornful looks at them and the clucking ceased.

"The very same battle that Jesus fought against Satan's demons on the plateau below Gergesa is being fought here again today," I continued. "It is simply another conflict between the forces of good and evil. Our divine, holy almighty God and Savior Jesus Christ was victorious on that day three centuries ago, and he will prevail here today. And just as happened on that day, the swine whom the demons possess will plunge over the cliff and perish in the abyss!"

At that a roar went up from the crowd of bishops, and the followers of Arius slipped quietly from the hall. The session was over for that day. I left the podium and went straight to my room.

Eusebius Again

A short time later, Eusebius tapped on my door and at my invitation entered. "I think your remarks today set the tone for the rest of the conference," he declared with a twinkle in his eye. "There's now talk of excommunication and possibly exile for Arius, Eusebius of Nicomedia and Theognis of Nicea and a few of their followers. If that Nicodemian is banished from the church, people won't mistake him for me anymore. And... you'll like this, my friend... in private conversation, the emperor characterized the uproar you caused as nothing less than the judgment of God."

"I think Christ's church now understands exactly who and what he is," I reflected. "Now our duty is to love each other, to forgive, to restore unity to the body, to witness to others and to get on with the business of feeding the hungry, clothing the naked, and tending the sick."

"I agree," he responded, "And I will make it my duty from this day on to use whatever influence I have to bring the brotherhood together again."

Soon thereafter the assembly unanimously adopted a creed declaring Jesus the Christ to be of one substance with the Father.

Cardinal Error

I need no clock nor clamorous cock
    To warn of dawn's arrival,
For when the sun peeps o'er the hill
    A little bird with giant will
    Whose only weapon is his bill,
I hear in mortal combat lock't,
    In battle for survival.

My picture window faces south,
    O'er view quite arboreal
And sets the southern border line
    For what the redbird says is mine
    And frames a nest in towering pine
From whence his lady ere doth mouth
    Her cardinal appeal.

But love must wait! The battles loom
    To save his lady's honor,
For in that window where I hide
    An image bird, yet bona fide,
    Reflected to and from his side,
Lurks in the shadow of my room
    And vaunts to leap upon her.

From dawn to dusk the furies pound,
Blow for blow and round for round,
A parry left, a parry right,
A lunge of equal length and might,
Every feint and thrust reversing,
Curses met with echo cursing.
Never gaining, never losing,
Only glass and self abusing,
Lust for battle yet unsated,
Mate awaiting waits, unmated.

Late the oak tree shadows mark
And banish rival bird to dark.
The hero of the mimic fray
Limps wounded on his nestward way
With aching wing and battered beak,
His soul and body far too weak
To raise the head of Cupid's pride
For sporting with his waiting bride.
He rushes off to tardy sleep
Too tired to hear his lady weep.

Cardinal Error

And all too soon dawn rudely roars
And calls him back to mirror wars.
Tell me, redbird, if you know,
Enchanted by so false a foe,
Will you ever comprehend
That light's rays are taught to bend?

Or are your senses now so shrunk
That like a pug who's gone punch drunk,
You'll flop around on my back lawn
When all your feathered friends have gone,
Driven by that sense sublime
To flee to more congenial clime?
From spring to fall the furies pound,
Blow for blow and round for round.

You'll perch atop my frozen gate
    To call in vain your missing mate,
    And mourn your self-inflicted fate.

When in the wind and swirling snow
    You seek your daily ration,
Will you ever come to know
    The destiny you fashion?

Her love for you you never fed;
    A siren suitor turned her head
    And lured her from your piney bed.

For honor, love and vast estate
> Have you stopped to count the cost?
You'll find when wars at last abate,
> You've only fought yourself, and lost.

Robert Sikkenga 1994

Ashes

Young Meyer Eich rode his bike
From Garden Inn to River Bend
To tend the crypt of Oberst Lipp.

From mother's knee with soldier's glee
The Oberst plucked the simple boy
And took him home to be his own
Frau Lipp's amusing garden toy.

He plundered precious family things:
Her father's watch and mother's stole;
He stripped her fingers of their rings
And seized the widow's golden bowl.

Frau Lipp, nee Steiner, kept the inn
Her parents willed her when they died,
And barren there she served the brew
That kept her husband's camp supplied

Amity Street

With all the *Geist* good soldiers need
To numb the sense and ease the bane
When God and country order them
To purge the land of evil strain.

As Meyer's tribe sank in the flood
Vistula's banks became his ark,
And unaware of any blood
He toiled in Lipp's botanic park,

A husbandboy to flowering shrubs,
Behind the privet doomed to groom
Mock orange, begonia, lilac, plum,
Rose of Sharon, furze and broom.

Near the coal stove in the shed
A wooden box became his bed,
And every day he earned his meat
Keeping Frau Lipp's garden neat.

Then late one June a filtered moon
Cast o'er the land a blotchy rash,
And morbid sky spread o'er the earth
A layer of the sooty Ash

That spewed from kilns the Oberst fired
To torch the earth's most undesired
And disinfect the land God spared
For Japheth's race, to go unshared.

Ashes

All summer long the Ash rained down;
It settled thick on yucca shoots,
Sank deep into the fertile ground
And gathered at the 'dendron roots.

Eich washed it from the windowpanes
And swept it from the bricken lanes;
He shook it from hydrangea limbs
And packed it neath the hyssop stems.

Then with the spring's refreshing rains,
As Ash surged through the greedy veins
Of Hawthorne, box and bridal wreath,
The nimbus martyred souls bequeath

To all creation lit the skies
Above that garden paradise
And filled the air with fragrant balm
That drugged the drowsy earth to calm.

Amid profusion Meyer toiled
And lopped and pruned and plied his art;
He swept up all the trimmings neat
And stacked them in his garden cart,

Hauled them off behind the shed
And piled them on the compost bed
Where rotting blossoms sadly bled
And mingled with the Ashen Dead

And household scum Frau Lipp had scraped
From pot and pan and dinner plate,
And bones and other dregs and orts
Left behind by sundry sorts.

Then droning shadows from the north
Rained fire to purge the purging land,
And Oberst Lipp, his courage flown,
Took his life by his own hand:

One day behind the garden shed
As Meyer crouched beneath the sash
Lipp put his Luger to his head
And fell among the fallen trash.

The widow bought a crypt of stone
At River Bend where Eich was shown
A golden bowl of ashes slipped
Into a niche marked "Oberst Lipp,"

And told his weekend task would be
To tend the lawn and linden tree
That grace the final resting place
Of this great hero of his race.

She placed the gate key in his hand
And charged to him the honored man
Who fell in duty to his land
And earned a monument so grand.

Ashes

Every morning she arrived
Just as the chapel bell tolled eight,
Knelt a moment in respect
And laid fresh flowers at the gate.

From forty-four to ninety-three,
Near half the bygone century,
She snipped the spirea bloom
And laid it at her husband's tomb.

From forty-four to ninety-three,
Near half the bygone century,
As Sabbath Eve laid shadows long,
Meyer gathered up the throng

Of flowers left at River Bend
And pedaled back to Garden Inn
To add his cargo to the Dead
That festered in his compost bed.

One cold fall day the tribute ceased;
Black crepe adorned the garden gate
Her soul had given up its lease;
Frau Lipp had joined her honored mate.

They took her ashes to the crypt
And poured them in the golden bowl
To rest forever in the niche,
Dust to dust and soul to soul.

Then on the last October day,
When Monday morning frost had nipped
The 'mums that grew around the crypt
Of Oberst and his good Frau Lipp,

Meyer took a broken stick
And churned a hole deep in the thickened
Rubble of his compost heap,
And while the lees began to seep,

Old Meyer Eich rode his bike
From Garden Inn to River Bend
To tend the crypt of Oberst Lipp.
As day poured out its final dole

Of sun, he took the golden bowl
And through the shadows of the night
He pedaled back toward the light
That he had hung beside the shed,

Then, just before he went to bed
He shook the ashes in the bowl
And poured them down
The compost hole.

Robert Sikkenga 1998

To order additional copies of

Have your credit card ready and call:

Toll free: (877) 421-READ (7323)

or please visit our web site at
www.pleasantword.com

Also Available at:
www.amazon.com
and
www.barnesandnoble.com

Printed in the United States
31961LVS00007B/88-129